FRAGILE II

Copyright © 2023 by A. Erin Walker

Cover image by Angela Ledyard Photography
Illustrations by Marissa McDowell

First Printing, 2023

All rights reserved. No part of this book may be reproduced in any manner whatsoever without written permission except in the case of brief quotations embodied in critical articles and reviews.

Published by Open Heart, an imprint of January Ave. LLC.

Fragile II

A. ERIN WALKER

January Ave.

For you.

Contents

IN LOVE

IN PAIN

Contents ~ ix

IN MOTION II

INSANE

IN MOTION I

time

I watch you disappear before my eyes,
How exhilarating it must be to fly,
As we stand exhausted by your speed,
You're a tough one.
We lose track and wonder where you've gone and you keep going.
No turning back,
No matter how much we ask,
No pausing moments we wish to last,
No skipping ahead to what's to come.
Just steadily moving at your pace and unraveling presents along the way,
Of disappointment or lust,
Fulfillment or piercing emptiness,
Satisfaction or love,
Or all of the above all at once.
Then as you continue to change we continue to change,

And the presents rewrap themselves in infinite
ways,
And we learn that your job is never to be con-
trolled,
But rather to show us the value in watching you go.

magic eyes

This type of vision can't be bought.
Not tunnel or laser,
Blank pages are still filled and karma is claim-
ing her kills.
The kind that pierces the facade, stunts the
outlying,
And saves a path from being led on.
It sees louder than the volume of words and
acts of grandeur covering ulterior matters.
It saves trust from insertion to hidden agendas,
And gifting a piece of a soul to the unwell and
hazardously unknown.
The type of vision that won't let one slip or fail,
That won't leave one low and dry,
Sipping fire from the wrong supply.

i am love, and i overflow

The power I wield could never be duplicated,
I am the embodiment of my ancestors' wishes.
I see what cannot be seen,
And feel what's impossible to touch.
I'll be selfish with myself over anything else,
I've never adored anything else so much.
But I am love, and I overflow.
I tend to overpour and overfeed,
Because I want everything to have everything it needs.
I give, and I give, and I live to give,
And never once think to receive,
Until I'm empty.
And I retreat.
And in solitude, I plant seeds and create new worlds,

I leave it all behind to save myself.

Because the one doing all the saving isn't saved by anyone else.

just go

How long is this ride?

It's already been a journey.

Being found in being lost but never once losing track,

The destination being in question but never once looking back,

How is that?

Just forced to trust that we're set to arrive on time every time,

Although we don't know where we're meant to go.

alone I

Content within my inner peace,
Preferring to go unseen,
Preferring not to be perceived.
Inhaling carefully cultivated energy,
Exhaling what doesn't resonate with me,
My happiest place.
Anywhere that I'm the keeper
Of the atmosphere,
And I order it to be still,
And just enjoy.

math-ing

What has crossed me was necessary,
Keys to different doors to different worlds,
It's meant for me to take my pick.
Led by lessons and blessings,
One different decision changes the entire trajec-
tory,
Guided to the greatest desires I've yet to know.
Long-awaited wishes incomparable to what's writ-
ten,
Multiply the monumental, the mystery,
Going back and forth on the misery,
Stepping back and forth between what's here and
what's on the horizon,
The future has me in a chokehold,
It's hard to stay present.
Add overwhelming anticipation,
And hundreds of hours sprouting to hundreds of
days in waiting,

And subtract patience.

the journey is lonely

Wasting so much energy on getting others to understand,
They're not meant to get it,
It's not meant for them.
^ Read that again.
A main character seeking approval from NPCs,
On a plan with a result only meant for you to see,
You've been chosen.
Second-guessing your position because the path is lonely,
Instant gratification of the cycle is calling,
The security of a predictable routine is enthralling,
But you're meant for so much more.
There must be so much more behind your choice to waste time,
Imagine being hand-picked,

Set to find and experience the meaning of life,
And you fumble.
Imagine being far too humble,
Convincing yourself you're like everyone else,
When everyone else is nothing like you.
They sleep soundly and don't remember their dreams,
They find contentment in doing the same old things,
You know you're not the same.
Your vision is your gift to give life,
You don't need them to believe with you,
You just need to believe in you,
And everyone will catch up the moment you see it through.

cancer moon

You crash against land,
Bearing needs tailored to me,
Previously unknown,
And unseen.
Weighted deliveries cause your aggression,
Light attempts gone unnoticed,
And rarely protected,
The job needed to get done.
Standing on the edge,
Locked into your depths,
I move with you,
Rushing waters to the surface as the sun approaches.
Hypnotizing long after messages are received,
You bring the ends of the world to its knees,
Influencing as far as the eyes can see,
And even farther.
Lost in you every time because I'm apart of you,

A connection that isn't new,
But the sparks are reintroduced,
When you reach my feet.
The moon admires you,
I entered the world with the moon in you,
Must be why you capture me so deep from inside,
And why everything they do is rarely taken in
stride.

now could be forever

Tomorrow is lost in the gray,
And so far away,
Now could be forever.
The breath of Mondays wishes for Fridays,
Spring daydreams about Fall,
We pretend time isn't all we have,
And proceed to give nothing our all.
Set to look back and just hope,
That we never said never to our personal treasure,
And did everything we could to never see regret.

77

Greater forces at play,
On this path towards enlightenment we're looking
both ways,
And the sky is falling.
Through the debris we see the future,
Our grasps loosen control.
All we need to know is where we want to go,
A new world is calling.
Our vibration has been awakened,
Our potential is lethal,
Our old lives don't stand a chance.

in motion

In a space both lacking and fulfilling,
A recalibration is needed.
A review for a focused mind battling an obstructed view,
It should all keep getting better.
Rose-colored lenses stained,
The route has never been pretty.
Romanticizing the struggles to stay sane,
Hoping to make it through faking it.
Meshed between comfort zones and unknowns,
I can't leave myself here.
Playing pretend through images out of fear,
And missing the courage to go.
These steps are getting heavy,
I see the temptation in falling back.
The enticing consolation of the past,
And the attraction to stagnancy is gripping.
What's left behind wants another chance,

To keep me as I am.
But the obsession with progression is endless.

bittersweet

Bittersweet.
When the inspiration won't let you sleep,
Lying awake engulfed in dreams,
Increasing salivation,
And melting on your tongue.
A taste too good to be true,
Leaving you hoping,
Obsessed with working,
Finding the recipe to guarantee,
It's on its way to you.

3 AM

The rain activates my mind,
The streets at 3 AM are calmer than the beating in my chest,
My body begs to rest.
My spirit craves adventures in alternate timelines,
But I've become one with the question marks and deafening silence,
And answers that only choose violence.
Intertwined with the darkness that only comes at night,
Visited by everything but peace.

more life

A piece of me left in peace of mind,
I've been calling for it ever since.
From one level to the next,
I'm hardly satisfied.
Not free enough,
I don't exhale enough,
I need less survival,
And more life.

lock in

You try your best not to allow the extra shit to get involved,
    Real life lies here.
    But one *'what if'* appears and knots form in your chest,
    You act out of fear.
    Get out of your head,
    Get into your heart.
    And discover the power in fusing them together,
    As you further learn to tell them apart.

you're right

It would've never crossed your mind if it wasn't
yours,
How many times will you let the details deter your
dreams?
Only you can ease the difficulty,
Choose to believe it's easier than it seems.
It's meant for you,
And will always be for you,
Just do it and see.
Instead of allowing what you don't know to oc-
cupy valuable space,
Instead of staying in the lane that's safe.
Putting yourself through pain that hasn't even
made itself plain,
If it comes true, focus in, but only then.
Until then,
The best thing to put yourself through twice,
Is the possibility of everything going right,

Proving yourself right.

perspective

How great are our cares,

In comparison to a moon so full it begs to be touched,

And travels to distant ocean floors yet to be explored.

Or ocean waves that scrape the sky, effortlessly stealing clouds,

And pools of stars shining bright sides on the darkness we rather hide,

Making paths to galaxies beyond galaxies,

Housing worlds within worlds,

With infinite beings and their finite cares and realities.

Our existence returns to humility,

Worries expose their triviality,

When the light behind eyes is revived.

divinely guided

My angels hear when I'm speechless,
Divinely guided and protected,
These days, it's best I speak less.
These days, it's more apparent how worries are
meaningless,
And external validation has no true basis,
All that matters lies inside.
The answers never left my possession,
I possess divinity, why seek worldly advice?
When I bear witness to the miracle that is my life
and my path,
Every day I make history,
With every step I expand a legacy,
I'm on my way.
What is there to prove by naming my every move?
The world will bear witness too,
I'll be there soon.

IN LOVE

love embodied

Each palm comforts the other,
Resting at the third eye to remind us to guide our thoughts,
And trust ourselves.
Then to our nose and lips to send love to our senses,
And note the importance of speaking things to existence.
Then to our hearts as a reminder that we are love embodied,
And we should love our entire selves from our minds to our bodies,
And see love in everybody.
Look at you,
God's greatest creation,
Living your greatest reincarnation.

the realest

My greatest peace has come
In relinquishing all that is not me.
Not pretending for the approval of others,
Not being present to appease with an act,
Not required to put on facades to attract,
This energy speaks for itself.
Their standards aren't hard to reach,
And it's not their standards I even seek.
Naturally impressive,
Alluring, endearing,
Intrinsically reassuring,
I live to impress me.
I won't overthink myself into some bullshit.
This authenticity is a gemstone,
With relieving properties to know
You'll never be fooled with mirrors,
Or suffocated with smoke.

venus in pisces

My goddess rules the deepest seas,
I thrive in fantasies.
Giving everything to fairytales,
And happy endings only truly alive inside.
Paying the fines to find consistency,
It is my pleasure.
The moon receives and generosity controls the weather,
Altruistic and protective when kept sacred and protected.
An ego birthed in ice spurs immense consideration,
Elusive and rarely obtained and never tamed.
With a world that is imaginative,
And a thawed heart that is compassionate,
When true love is to blame.

alone II

The mood is curated for greatness,
There is no mistaking it.
The air is peaceful,
The water is fine,
The energy is all mine.
My shoulders rest easy here,
My nerves are protected,
No other competition is as great for you,
As is my solitude.
My space, my safety, my one–woman tribe,
Wherever I am alone can be home.
If I can love your presence as much as mine,
You can be mine.

memories in love

You're in love with the fantasy,
Enticing and passionate,
And like fire it cannot be tamed,
But you're warmed by the flame.
The eyes pierce inside and you effortlessly spill your truths,
You uncontrollably fall in love,
Unapologetically express what it already knew,
Because it feels it too.
This moment we want to possess,
But it only lives as long as it allows,
Before reality drops us back down.
This connection radiates in fleeting scenes,
We paint The Town red with gold fronts and blue jeans,
A perfect dream.
Conversations dig deep and carry us to the morning,

We blink and the sun peaks into our world,
And we wish all nights could look like this and last forever.
We are the fantasy and the reality and you've fallen in love with one,
But what happens when the other one comes?
When the sun rises and tired eyes can only look back on memories,
When you're forced to question whether it's really as good as it seems.
Do I love you or what you've exposed to me?
Do you love the moment or me?

bedtime

Always here and always waiting,
Your loyalty works wonders.
I don't know where I would be without you,
Without your peace, your comfort,
Your unmoving ability to make it all better,
Or breathe life into the perception that everything
is alright.
You refresh me,
Without pressure, you undress me,
I'm happy to remove it all for you.
I'm happy to climb in without my armor,
I release what consumed me from the day,
And hate the moment I have to walk away,
The departure is never easy.
With the unpredictability between good morning
and good night,
Your consistency is key,
You heal me after facing the world,

You mean the world to me.
I'm blessed to have you as the star of my sacred
space,
   Not many deserve what you provide,
   That's why not just anyone can come inside,
   That's why you make it so hard to say goodbye.

cologne

Deep in warm reactions,
Stretches and pulsations,
Senses reaching far beyond satisfaction.
This home is yours,
Your smile is my throne.
Our souls mate through fingertips
And hushed moans,
And cracked screens and heated phones,
You emanate from my skin and the sheets,
You'll be back.
I breathe you in as I wait,
Even when alone,
I'm never alone.

safe space

With you,
I'm walking on the moon without leaving this room.
Right where I need to be,
My scars are slowly disappearing.
As I wander in us,
I can't help but think,
This must be what it means to be free.
To lock eyes with a spirit and find no limits,
To melt into one without worries of what's to come.
To find the best of everything fitting into the little things,
Glowing from joy,
Knowing I'll never fall,
Knowing I won't lose myself if I give my all.
Even if only until the scars are healed,
Or only to help return my smile,

You're pleased to be exactly what I need,
My safe space for a while.

disrobe

Call me whatever you want,
Call this whatever you want,
Just keep calling.
I like to release the weight of a name,
The pressure that comes with titles,
Placing convenience in placing blame.
Just keep coming back and don't change,
And this will always be the same.
I'll always be here for deep-rooted laughter,
And other worldly discussions.
Just stay open with me for a while,
Just stay for a while.
You can remove your shield for a while,
I'm all in.

magick

Red wine seeps into the plush, white rug. The lipstick painting the rim of the glass is cracked.

With every rhythmic bump against the coffee table, the other creeps closer to the edge.

And with every thrust she moans life into his mouth. Using their passion to fuel the transformation of dream lives to reality. They envision their greatest successes as he enters and exits. The second glass falls.

Her panties rest on the floor beside his shirt. A trail of layers removed when the tension heightened the mood. The music channels their nature, she humbly takes control.

Staring into his soul, one hand on his heart, the other gripping his neck, his eyes widen as he digs his fingers into her waist.

"You're so beautiful," he says. "I'm so proud of

you... you're the woman you've always wanted to be..." she looks to the ceiling.

"Look at me," he growls. She reunites with his eyes.

"You feel so good," she utters. "I'm so grateful for you... the best protector, the best teacher, the best lover..." he brings a hand behind her neck and their torsos meet before their lips.

And they embody their words in images of their perfect life in perfect worlds in shared eruptions, their future is locked in.

goodbye is an illusion

Crying from goodbyes until my heart saved my mind,
"You forgot that leaving is deceiving,
Our tie is forever".
What is shared is not reliant upon temporary vessels,
I wish I could recall the memories of everyone we are.
Losing and finding each other through every time-line,
Forgetting we're infinitely connected,
Forgetting I don't have to panic about finding the other half of my soul,
You'll always show.
Then I cry about letting go,
When it should be nothing to wait until next time,

Since we're accustomed to waiting lifetimes,
It's never truly goodbye.
No matter how far we go,
We'll always share another hello.

the universe is in love with me

It's not crazy,
How everything tends to work in my favor,
That's what happens when you're favored.
When your frequency defaults to gratitude and miracles,
I choose to align with what I want from this life,
I'm here for a reason.
To breathe out, and breathe in,
And let go of every season,
To make room for the best to come in,
And have something beyond this world to believe in.
And believe I'm beyond this world,
That's why I can't blend in.
That's why I'm disconnected from the narrative,
And intrinsically connected to the collective,

Why I have to be alone to feel protected,
I know my experience.
And I know it's fueled by love and peace,
And I'm here to make my way back to me.
And every right path will travel easy,
Because the universe is in love with me.

forever

Relax with me
Under jazz soundtracks dancing
With weighted eyelids.

Fingers follow the lifelines
Inside of palms
Between soft kisses.

The air of the future glistens.

Move confidently in the truth
of what forever means to you.

heavy

A heavy heart turns a heavy head,
I might not sleep tonight.
I might be everywhere but here,
The vessel lies clear as the spirit is elsewhere.
I swear,
It doesn't take much for my mind to run amok.
It doesn't take much for me to lose my sense of touch,
But I've met a crutch.
Lifting me up,
Ensuring I continue to feel,
Testing me after fake encounters making sure I know what's real,
I know you're real.
Because these sleepless nights can bring no armored knights,
All I see is what's in front of me.
No waking to find it's all in my mind,

You're a dream without reverie a character of my reality,
That's insanity.
How I'll be tossing restless over and over,
Subconsciously fighting slumber,
When drenched with precious thoughts how my cup runneth over.
What you're presenting is becoming bolder and bolder,
I'm enticed and enamored,
I don't want to turn over.
I want to keep my mind from running clear,
I want you to keep living there.
I don't want to sleep at night when you hold me in real life,
I just wanna breathe in your essence and talk less,
A heavy heart turns a heavy head I shall remain restless.

release

Release your inhibitions,
Take off your expectations.
Rarely flattering and never fitting as they should
be,
You'd be better off without these.
Because your mind can be persuasive,
Illusions of fear abrasive.
Sometimes it's hard to hear what your intuition
has to say,
When it whispers deep within to follow your faith.
The logic may have argued this isn't the time nor
place,
Yet here we lie,
After many days and nights,
Still loving and being loved.
We can't make sense of everything,
We can't keep getting in our own way,
Just because what we hope for is initially unseen,

We don't have to see and feel to believe,
Just release.

present

A message missed in the midst of all this.
Chaos kicked up gravel from the pavement,
Stretched hearts with desperate ears waited,
Most bodies remained buried in distance,
While others emerged in reacquaintance.
Unblock me from your present,
All this shit is too hectic.
This moment might really be our last,
So just spend what you can,
With me.
Making up for the time we've lost,
All the time I spent banished to your past.
Waves of whispers carry uncertainty of what's to
come,
Between these four walls,
We build our own freedom.
We illustrate our own way to get away,
And your breath whispers that you've missed me.

I would have never heard it from under the ground,
I feel bad for being thankful,
That the world flipped upside down.

you're invited

Locked within myself,
Between abstract walls and transparent ceilings,
Large windows with attractive views,
Made just for me,
But always open for you.
My body called,
My heart took the night off.
Pin me against the skyline,
Glowing under the red lights,
Sweating shea butter and coconut,
And recovering every drop on our tongues.
A smile will wake me up,
And the morning makes my heart pretend,
It knows nothing of what happens,
When the night comes.

conflicted

I yearn for you,
Without knowing what I yearn for,
Pacing the floor,
Searching my mind,
Hoping to find more.
More about what it is that I need,
And why it disagrees with what I feel,
Because you're ready to move into something real,
But I'm at a standstill.
I'm not ready to be placed there with you,
Wanting all that you do,
Although I want it too,
Just, not now.
I know it will unfold to what it's meant to be,
Without interference from you or me,
There is no we,
Just You and I,
And time.

And respect as we strive not to rush what's grow-
ing inside,
    And the more it consumes,
    The less I'll hide.
    Let's hold off as long as we can,
    While what I want and what I need,
    Grow to go hand in hand.

experience

The experience that is you continues.
Everything is brightened,
Senses heightened,
And consistently breathing you in.
As days go no longer saved,
Sleeveless, golden nights turn silver under duvets,
The experience that is you continues.
Without suppression, insecure possession, nor just something to do,
But rather all that is open, freeing, cherished,
And beyond more than what I hoped for.

flashbacks

Eyes drifting toward skylights
In a journey through highlights.
The charge from your fingertips
Loves to shock me then reel me in,
What lies in my deepest fantasies,
Please be the one to fill me in.
Because your skin on mine ripples light waves
through my veins,
That gaze into my eyes while you're inside
Makes the grip tighter between my thighs,
Are you surprised?
Because I tell you all the time how I want this all
the time,
And I can't go a moment without it on my mind.
And the electricity you've sparked in me is fused
into you,
So as my soul is charged by memories, your soul
feels it too.

fwb's always fall
in love

Here for sex and safe connection,
Too light for higher expectations,
Too closed for the anticipation of deception,
This ice is a weapon when the rules aren't clear.
But here, it's just enough to keep from feeling but staying touched,
And receiving without giving too much.
We link up inside each other's minds,
Our smiles are good friends,
Our bodies entangle to no end,
And your world knows no danger,
But the background is always ticking.
There is always a timer on the illusion of understanding,
Change will always make its way.
One day the heart will want to play,

This arrangement is cozy and safe,
Love is dying to live here.
The rules blur with unspoken requests,
The normal meeting spot has moved,
We don't know exactly where we are but share
unspoken respect,
We don't know exactly what we are but won't be
the one to ask,
Won't be the one to risk putting whatever we have
in the past,
Just let it last.
For however long it's meant to last,
Even if meant to end in pain,
Let it enjoy the illusion of love,
Without counting the days.

angel

Another wild day on Twitter. Another main character making a fool of themselves. We all know not to be that person.

I silently laugh at my phone, only glancing upward to ensure I'm heading in the right direction.

The scent of pretzels taunt me as I pass Auntie Anne's. I might have to double back later. But for now, the mission is candles. And maybe shower gel. Bath & Body Works is having a sale and the sale is calling my name.

I click on a video posted on the Twitter timeline and unbeknownst to me it's very sexual and very loud and my earphones are in my ears but not turned on, they're just there for decoration. The moaning sounds echo around me as I swipe them away and my chest hurts. I scan the area for anyone sending judgment for my mistake, and make eye contact with another young woman. She's heading in my direction. I keep my pace, looking back down to my phone and-.

"Hey!"

I glance back up and she is now directly in front of me. We both come to a stop. She's very smiley. I frown at her apparent excitement to see me, and rack my brain for her face in any memories but there are no results. I place my earphones in my bag.

"Hello..."
"How are you? I love your jacket."

I look at the sleeve of my plaid jacket with various tones of brown draped over my body. A great find from the thrift store with a very visibly ripped pocket that grows every year. "I'm fine... thank you?"

I don't want to be rude, but I start back walking, hoping she'll notice I'm on the move and let me be, but she joins my stride. "I have one just like it," she says. Still smiling. Still excited.

"Does it have a ripped pocket too?" I gesture to the eyesore and she laughs.

"No, but it has seen better days."

I nod. She stops walking but continues to look at me, I don't want to be rude. I stop walking too and look over my shoulder as well as behind hers, is she distracting me from something? Is someone going to run up and rob me? Or does she want to sell me something, what the hell does she want? I'll just excuse myself. "Well, I have to get going."

"Are you doing some shopping?"

Now, I know she sees the confusion on my face. I could hide it until this moment. Why is she speaking to me? Why me? Do I seem like the "nice" type? The type of girl you strike up random conversation with mid-walk in the middle of the mall? What is the point?

"Yes, just a little..."
"What store?"
"Bath & Body Works..."
"Oh wow, I was heading that way too."

I nod, deciding not to speak on her blatant lie,

and she doesn't break eye contact or end her smile. Okay...? Am I supposed to...? Okay. Fine.

"Want to walk there with me?"

"Yes, let's go!" the question barely leaves my mouth before she accepts.

She continues to strike up conversation about random topics as we walk, hardly carrying them and forcing me to find words to participate. The amazing scents of our destination reach our noses and we accept baskets from a smiling associate at the entrance. She follows as I peruse tables of candles. I remove various tops, sniff, and either place it back on the table or place the selection in my basket. The ones I like, she asks to smell too. She follows me and we do the same with shower gels. Then, I decide to be satisfied with what I've collected, trying not to be frustrated that my solo shopping trip has been ambushed by a stranger. "I'm gonna go get in line," I say.

"Okay, me too."

Of course.

I notice her basket is empty. "You didn't see anything you wanted?"

"No, not this time."

We stand in line and she's visibly distracted. She keeps looking over her shoulder. My shoulders tense. This feels off. What is she planning? Why do I have to be so concerned about being perceived as rude to the point where I'm putting my life in danger by letting this strange woman latch on to me? She's definitely going to rob me. Or worse. I don't even know. I don't even want to think about it.

The line moves and I step forward and she steps forward too, but now she is texting something on her phone. My heart is racing. She has to be letting her partners in crime know we're about to be on our way out the store. What could be waiting for me when I walk outside? My eyes strain to read what she types while keeping my face forward, but to my surprise, she moves closer so her arm is against mine and tilts the screen in my direction.

You're being followed. Don't look now. Man in green jacket, black baseball cap. He's standing outside, waiting.

My breathing struggles. It's hard not to look now. She deletes the note and starts typing again. The line moves. I hardly step forward, on edge waiting for her next message.

Act normal. I'll walk with you to your car. We'll be okay.

"Next!" the cashier calls.

I checkout my items that suddenly seem so inconvenient and unnecessary and we head toward the exit. I briefly catch sight of the man she described and she strikes up another conversation, calling me back to "acting normal". I do my best to find words and participate and hide the trembling of my hand as I use the camera on my phone to pretend to check my hair while actually looking behind me. Green jacket and black cap is still trailing. We approach the escalator that leads down to the sunless parking garage. He's talking on the phone, his eyes on the back of my head. I turn off the camera.

"What if he-," I begin to panic.
"He won't," she interrupts. "We're okay."

I wish her confidence would fill me up as we let the escalator take us down. I refuse to check if he's still behind us as as our surroundings dim. I keep my taser in the glove compartment of my car, and right now I'm pissed about that. What is it supposed to do for me in there?

I want to power walk through the garage but she keeps her same pace, so I stay beside her. I keep freaking myself out, imagining someone reaching for me from behind but the contact never comes. Every step to my car builds greater anticipation, it feels like I parked miles away. She keeps assuring me with her eyes that we'll be okay.

Once I reach the driver's side, the relief quickly subsides as she stands at the passenger door. I hesitate to unlock the car. She could be lying. She could have successfully lied her way into being led to my car, that man could be her partner. "I should be fine from here," I say.

"Trust me," she says.

I take a deep breath and my first mind presses the button to unlock the door before the fears could follow. She gets in and I do too. She hits the locks once we're inside and I put my shopping bag in the back and cut on the engine.

"My car is just over there," she points toward the next row over.

I see the green jacket and black cap standing at the bottom of the escalators, scanning the garage and seeming to be searching for us with no luck. I take another deep breath. "It looks like we lost him somehow. How did you know he was following me?"

"When I first saw you, he was tailing you pretty closely and staring at you. He looked nervous, I could tell something was wrong."

"That's why you started talking to me."

"Exactly."

"And here I thought you were just being polite," sarcasm tries to cover the anxiety. The man finally heads back up the escalators and I put the car in reverse to back out of the parking spot.

She laughs. "Oh, you didn't find the random conversation with a stranger weird? Like maybe I was trying to rob you?"

My smile subsides. "Actually..." we both laugh. "I hate how crazy this world is. I wish you could take someone's kindness for face value. You just never know what people are really up to."

"Thankfully, your intuition isn't of this world. And you listened to it."

I turn down the next row of cars.

"That's mine right there, the white one," she points. I stop in front of the vehicle. "Promise me you'll pay more attention to your surroundings, sis."

"I will. I definitely will. I think I'll do a lot of things differently after today," I force a smile. "Thank you so much for doing what you did. I really might owe you my life."

She smiles back and opens the door. I watch as she walks around the front of my car and arrives at the driver's side of hers and gives one last wave. I look down at the gear shift, my hand pausing before putting the car back in drive.

She just helped me. I feel like I owe her. The least I can do is maybe get her a pretzel sometime.

I press the button to lower my window. "Hey, maybe we should-," but she's no longer there. I look inside the white car but it's empty.

I hurriedly send the window back up and smash the locks, my eyes rapidly scanning the surround-ings of the garage all around my car for any sign of her or any sign of anyone, but there is no one. Just as quickly as she appeared and just as easily as she saved me, she disappeared.

favored

Out of all the stars I'll only wish upon you.
You've turned wishes to realities,
Immersed me in victories,
Saved me from tragedies,
You're one of one and I'm grateful.
Grateful to know and love you,
Grateful you know and love me,
I give thanks every day.
Because my path could have been much different,
But you've never ceased to guide and show me much better ways.

safe haven

Carefully curated safety and magic,
Born from the law of attraction,
My mind made this happen.
This is a sanctuary.
Right here you can be who you are,
You can unwind from the day,
You can recharge,
And hide from the world.
Spiritually cleansing the energy and regulating it
with love,
My ancestors protect the threshold,
No ill intentions survive here,
Pure hearts call it a vibe.
Home is where the heart is,
I put my heart into my home,
Grateful to set the tone,
Grateful to guarantee peace.

thank you

Partly sunny,
Immersed in thought clouds,
Thinking out loud.
I found you and I'm proud and I'm smiling.
I don't know what's meant to come of this or where we're meant to go,
Or who we're meant to be,
But one of my favorite things about you is you're down for anything.
Thanks for being a supporter and major stress-reliever,
An angel showering me with kisses and best wishes,
Ready to ride the long way,
I really fuck with you the long way.
Because while my mind is usually high in the clouds,
You give my spirit a joyful reason to roam free,

But also manage to keep my feet on the ground.

rays

My skin drinks your love,
My hair grows to you,
You burn for me,
I honor you.
For someone that finds solace in the night,
I look to your light as much as the moon,
I sit on time for your set,
And pray for your rise.

what aren't we?

I don't want to take you from you,
I won't initiate anything that facilitates the loss of
your essence,
When combining with mine.
I just want to dive into the experience,
And let it move us.
I asked for only the greatest intentions to be wel-
come in my home,
So guests are far and few,
It's really only you,
But you're still my favorite.
You make it easy to run away from sleep,
To travel deep into the night and feel your body
near me,
To not miss the moment when I'm pulled in closer,
I'll stay here forever as long as it's with you.
Whatever you're here to do, I'm here to do too.

whipped

Holding onto what remains near and dear,
As distance grows greater,
Between the cons and pros I used to know.
Your presence drives the migraines away,
My simplest pleasure,
The best reason to look forward to every day.
What else is out there,
Where else could I be privy to go,
Nowhere compares to right here,
There's no way I'll ever go away.
When in love,
I only care about whose heart calls me home,
And how much I'd love to stay.

some days

I run away to the ocean,
Hiding in mystery,
There I thrive,
There I come alive.
Losing connection externally,
Reconnecting internally,
Digging deeper into me.
Unexplored waters,
Sinking into unanswered questions,
What version of me is present?
Some days,
I crash against the shore with the waves,
Releasing bubbles and gliding wherever the wind
sways,
Some days I am who I am.
Some days I ride the tide and dive under,
Claiming lost cities and painting wonders,
Some days I am who I am.

palms at night II

And for a while,
It all stands still.
Gliding under blurred beams,
The top down,
The volume up,
We feed music to the night.
The road has your eyes and I forget about mine,
I become one with the breeze.
Cut the engine and realize,
The world is asleep,
We're no longer a part of it.
Called to feel the moon on our skin,
Our feet guess the distance to the edge,
Locked arms on dirt paths,
We hold each other at the vista.
Gazing at a big city,
Discussing big dreams,
And all of the lights,

And what it all means.
Above silhouettes of palm trees,
Guarded by stars,
This moment,
This night,
Is ours.

message of
intention

I haven't always been honest to who I am.
Only the shadows could reveal how much I break
promises.
I'm nicer to the world than I am to myself,
I tell myself what I'm going to do,
And once I see possibility to lose,
I don't pull through.
I don't even give myself a chance.
Lies fill my mind,
They help me sleep at night.
They say I do everything I commit to,
That I love me, and me loves me too,
But it's not fully true.
Self-love is a journey and there is no end.
I'll always grow and change,
I'll never stay the same,

Old versions of me wash away with the rain,
New versions arrive with every new day.
After all these years,
I'm just scratching the surface of getting to know,
Who I swore I've always known.
I'll always be on my way,
But at least I'm en route.
At least I'm working to trust myself,
At least I'm destined to love and be loved,
At least I've come far in arriving to myself.
At least I can admit I'm not there and I'm not perfect,
But I have the intent,
To truly fall in love with me.

IN PAIN

it's not you,
it's me

It's not about you,
It's about forcing something that is not meant to fit,
This situation isn't it.
You stick to the bare minimum,
Remaining nonchalant about us,
While outside players beg to be in your position,
Going above and beyond to give the max.
And I'm sorry,
But everything changed when I realized that.
I shouldn't have to ask and only receive when I'm ready to leave,
I should have known you weren't so clueless to what I deserved,
I should have believed I deserved it more.
I've never asked for too much,

I just wasn't courageous enough,
I believed the excuses were enough,
It's not about you.
It was never about you,
It's about me accepting anything just to have something,
Instead of facing the fear of loneliness,
For the chance to be found by something that fits.

you can never come back

She was way above the clouds trying not to look down,

Gazing forever forward, no desire to revisit all that's been left in the past,

There's a reason none of it was able to last,

It's beneath her, completed, removed, to her decision she's steadfast.

The stress isn't needed,

Anything that has to pretend must come to an end,

They would always know what to say to get back in but never again.

If you can't look in her eyes and see the sun,

Or look in her heart and see the one, your time is done.

No opportunity to bring darkness, her light is her pride and joy,

No risking what keeps her alive for someone that only sees a toy.

It's all fun and games until you're left speechless in mixed messages,

Racking your brain to make sense out of nonsense,

Purposely blinded by love's imposter, climbing out of dark voids,

Finding the path with your hands, sightless and struggling to understand,

Rising back to the light you never thought you'd feel again,

Reuniting with the sky you thought you'd never see again,

They don't know what it takes to make it out of that.

They'll never be freed from the past.

empty again

Constantly landing on empty by giving more than receiving,
I refill myself and repeat,
And it's fine.
I'm owed nothing.
And giving because that's what it means to be me,
I don't expect it to be you.
It would just be nice to experience the green grass on your side.

broken cords

Saturn said anyone questionable will have to go,
And was tired of repeating itself.
I'll still hold on knowing something is better suited elsewhere,
Will still cry when something I know should be removed is actually removed.
Leaning out of active denial and into painful acceptance,
This is where realizations and the truth orbit like the moon.
Years of imbalance gone unseen,
No one speaks on love in friendships being blinding,
How you can constantly pour and they constantly receive,
And you begin to believe it's natural to anticipate storms,

And natural to always make yourself available to their infinite victim role,

And natural to be a dumping ground,

They load and unload, load and unload,

And when it's your turn you never feel more alone.

Or because you act out of love you shouldn't be heartbroken when returns come up short,

Until the depletion is felt,

And an audit is conducted,

And you see how much of your energy has been abducted,

And how easily you were left with nothing,

If you care about me too, why is there always an excuse?

Our time is up.

I hope you find genuine connections that align,

Just as I'm hopeful I'll find mine.

My ruling planet has spoken,

I call all of my energy back to me safely and wish you well,

But this cord is broken.

villain

There's always three sides and this isn't about mine,

I hope you're relieved I don't just see what I want to see.

That I make space to analyze and refine and reflect on reflexes,

Lucky for you I'm one of a kind.

I know I'm the villain in your story.

Motives asked to be masked as mistakes,

Chances begged with tears and you gave them away,

I always knew what to say,

I always knew how to put you in your place,

And maybe that's what kept you in play.

You gambled all your chips away seeking my heart,

All the while set to lose from the start.

Unlike me you only see what you want,

So you came with your static perception,

Seeing and vowing to conquer,
Romanticizing reality was your weapon,
You never loved me.
You were in love with a thought,
And I sold you the dream you needed,
To get what I want.

media madness

I'm a mess of teardrops and smiles,
Hidden in piles of pillows and blankets submerged in seas of highs and lows,
I try really hard to keep the world separated from my soul.
If I let every catastrophe inside of me,
I wouldn't last,
The storms would never pass,
I have to protect myself.
They aim to keep us frightened and needy,
They fight to keep us mindless and binging,
Squeezing subliminal messaging behind the bigger picture
To strengthen the bigger picture,
Go figure.
No wonder our thoughts don't know which way to go,

No wonder it feels shameful to want to keep your
eyes closed,
Please remove the agenda.
Please know I'll never believe in the stories skewed
over me,
I'll never take their word over what I clearly see,
They'll never have control over me.

less and more

Left on read or begging for space,
Rarely on the same page,
Rarely able to gauge,
Why all the air is uncertain.
Ready to throw out the magnifying glass,
And hide in the shadows,
And hope it's in the plan,
For someone to have no fear of the dark.
The little patience that was left has left,
Splashed across the opposite wall,
Seasoned with the last sweet nectar of hope,
What remains is bitter,
That future I once loved to envision is dimmer.
Loyal to a thorough search,
Just to find,
Results consistently unable to provide,
A heart that beats in my direction without question.

Remove me from the cycle,
Subjected to actions on someone else's time,
Nonchalant reactions to missing replies,
The ego is persuasive,
It says I don't mind,
Pay it no mind.
Remove me from the cycle,
Subjected to pressure,
To commit to aspiring guarantees,
Unsure of how it even seems,
But promising that time won't be wasted,
In pursuit of what's long-awaited,
Even when I know I don't have energy to give,
As much as I did before.
Choking on the misery in mystery,
Buried in pretend solace of the shadows,
Craving both less and more.

waiting games

How did you miss me before?
Because my eyes always saw the prize in you,
While through yours, I was invisible.
Maybe you were distracted,
Maybe you were still enthralled by bad habits,
Maybe something or someone was better at catch-
ing your eye,
There must be a reason I was cast aside.
The question is hypothetical,
I know you'll just lie.
You only find loving me convenient,
It comes and goes on your time,
Only find me worthy of seeking when you see I'm
doing fine,
Your radar on my wellbeing torments my mind.
You take advantage of my weakness desiring love,
Wishing you'd be the prince of my fairytale,

Showing me bits and pieces to believe it can all
be there,
And I fall every time.
Because the urge to prove I can be more for you
loves to overshadow the truth,
And here we are.
I know I'll regret what I choose,
I know if you win that means I lose,
But after all we've been through,
The prize on the other side is no longer you,
We'll all see I was always right.

safe in the gray

The way you sit on my mind unread is unnerving.
I need to know if I should archive you.
I need to be set straight on your mixed messages,
Sent and unsent,
But I'm scared.
You know what you're doing in silence. You know what you're doing in the withholding of clarification,
I know how it feels to be both misled and misguided,
I just hate to remember.
I'd much rather forget.
I'd much rather be hopeful that sometimes,
Experience is a lie.
Another failed flame will leave me permanently cold.
I'd rather wait, unsure and unsettled in the gray.

not interested

It's hard pulling a loner out their comfort zone,
You beg for quality time because I'm happy being alone,
And I can't directly tell you to prove yourself worth my presence because it's rude,
Although the world claims to love and welcome the truth,
It's rare people actually do.
If I told you how much I love and appreciate myself,
And I find it hard to give attention to anyone else,
Because most of you are disappointing,
Always coming up short,
Hardly interesting,
Often annoying,
Hardly can afford what I can provide on my own,
Yet sense the disinterest in my tone and still won't let it go, why?

At least I impress myself,

At least I know I don't need to wait on someone else to experience wealth,

At least someone allowed to access my energy will always know how much they mean to me,

And how special they are,

Because these days,

People rarely make it that far,

Call me scarred.

Or call me smart.

To learn from experience and do the opposite,

To go against what once was and where it led me,

And take pride in what it all helped me to become,

I am literally the one.

And I'll only make time for my soul's equal,

The one that inspires my growth and motivates my drive,

The one that makes me feel alive.

But I can't say this because it's rude,

So I'll tell you to get this book and turn to page one hundred and two.

fomo

You should've known this was here.
It's been present all along,
Just waiting for you to notice.
Waiting for you to hear it,
Waiting for you to see.
Crazy how your eyes can be open and closed at the same time,
How you can respond so gracefully to something you weren't listening to.
You should've known about it,
It was loud and clear.
No subtleties or hints,
It fought with fear to catch a flight to your ear.
It was yours all along,
And you failed to claim.
Or you failed to care,
Could you at least care to explain?

Even if it has nothing left to utter but how much you're missing out,
It's unfortunate without a doubt,
How much you're missing out,
You're missing out.

consequences

I'll leave you alone.
I know you hate when I call upon the thunder.
And my face is wet from the sky's tears,
And the dirt behind your fingernails has morphed into mud,
Wash your hands,
And leave me out in the cold.
Because it's all up to you and I don't deserve your warmth.

shifted

The art of convenience has driven me up a wall,
I can't find the balance.
I can't escape the madness that ensues when
thinking about this situation and you.
I tend to give out many chances,
They're placed in others' hands and they thank me,
And I thank myself,
But maybe my generosity is the problem.
A lot of the effort exerted is less because they're
worth it,
But more to prove to myself I am not a monster.
I am willing to forgive and understand,
And not hold on to the past,
I do everything to make things last,
Especially when they don't go according to my
plan.
I would always fight for my way and told myself I
had to learn how to deal and bend,

The journey may not look how I prefer,
All that matters is reaching the desired end.
So I became less focused on idealizing and more on conceptualizing all possibilities,
Said I'll try everything at least once before concluding what's not meant for me,
I would bend and bend until one day I realized, the overcompensation to prevent me from being static and uncompromising was more in favor of the other side than myself,
I dived into discomfort and drained gallons of peace to accommodate someone else.
And there was no return besides resentment,
No desired end,
Of my imagination it was just a figment.
As the love story became so altered in attempts to be fair,
The love story for me was no longer there.
I know it was just convenient for you because I made it that way,
And it will never be that way again,
I'll never even be in a situation that requires me to bend,
Won't even entertain anyone that doesn't already fit the description,
Now the lack of balance has shifted.

imperfect punishment

I didn't mean what I said when I was healing,
And I don't mean to make it seem as if my process has ended,
No matter how much I would love to feel love again.
Solitude has become my home,
I feel safest when I'm alone,
But I know that's the trauma talking.
I dream of finding safety outside of myself,
This last bit of hope is all I have left,
I won't let it go yet.
The scars are fading but the pain is still haunting,
I want to let my guard down but it all still taunts me,
I can't let my trauma be contagious.
I can't seek love selfishly as if I'm not jaded,

I refuse to hurt the way I've been hurt.
There's no way to have you right now without
breaking you,
   And I want you to live,
   I need you to live.
   And I pray when my healing ends, we can try again.
   I would love to risk it all again,
   To feel love again.
   Risk the pain again,
   To feel that way again,
   One day I'll let my heart back out to play.

empathic and tragic

I cry often.

Tears bred from raw smiles, racking of nerves, and sharp chest pains,

Inflicted softly and harshly.

Digging,

Pulling waters from the depths,

An effect of feeling deeply.

Experiences of others booked first class to be mine,

The shoe may not always fit,

But I can wear it every time.

It's natural,

For me to consider you,

And imagine if you were me.

Probably why it's hard to see you sleeping on the same thing,

Hard to fathom the effects of your causes
Not being a part of your thinking.
But you're not who I'm blessed and cursed to be,
Although in the blink of an eye I can surely be you,
So I cry often,
While your tears fall far and few.

stuck at the
surface

Dazed off the paint of fragile lips,
Volatile, inviting butterflies with highs and dips,
Whichever way blows the wind.
Learn to speak another language,
Aiming for understanding in the watering of admiration.
An end to seeking love without the soil from which it comes.

letting go

My hand immediately regrets letting go,
You're trying to put this on hold,
Trying to promise you'll be back but I know better
than that.
I know I can come on strong,
I know I can be too hot or too cold,
These games we're forced to play are not for me.
I gain life from having someone to love,
Someone to hold,
Someone to call home,
I don't do well with pretending,
I won't lie and say I'm fine sleeping alone.
And maybe that's too much for you, and that's
disappointing.
It's disheartening to see a future refuse to involve
me,
Exhausting to see another lover turn their back,
The Pattern tells me to tighten up.

To quit placing potential on pedestals,
But my intrusive thoughts are fairy tales,
And I don't put them there.
I don't choose to care... the way I do,
I just do.
But I refuse to believe there isn't someone that will too.
Changing the way I nurture may unsubscribe me from this torture,
But I can't decrease the peace within me.
If I believe any less in the love for which I breathe,
How will the universe know I'm ready?
That I'm open to receive?
Someone to appreciate this passion,
Someone to honor me.
Someone to see the world in my eyes,
Be that release from disappointment,
The one unafraid of being loved always in all ways,
You're one my hand hates to let go of.
Our happy ending was supposed to be so sweet,
I hate that I won't taste it.
I hate that it won't be you.

late

I hate waiting.
Could go on but can't move on anticipating
The decision of a heart that's not my own.
Distance growing in delay,
Patience left a note on their way away,
And listed more reasons to uproot than to stay.
Sometimes we hope for surprises of new outcomes,
Playing for company in punctuality just to drift off alone.
How hard is it to speak your mind?
How hard is it to value the treasure you find?
Taking advantage until access is no longer granted,
How hard is it to water the seed you planted?
Only breaking a sweat when the temperature drops on being mine,
How hard is it to love someone on time?

out of my world

There's no place for you in my world anymore,
Matter of fact,
There was never a place for you before,
Good disguise.
Lucky you, I'm not the best to discern,
Lucky me, I still had lessons to learn,
Your evil eye and backhanded support meant so much more.
Spirits like yours are why I avoid all by choice,
I don't know who means it when they say they mean me well,
I don't know who anyone truly is and who sent them,
I'm still working on my intuition,
So I want nothing from anyone but space.
Don't want to trust or distrust,
Don't want to mistake competition for sisterhood,
If I have to get to know someone new,

I'm good.

Exhausted from being misunderstood and constantly misunderstanding,

Desiring healthy connection is too demanding,
It shouldn't be this hard.

you should know better

You don't know who you're dealing with and it shows,
Tell on yourself some more,
I spot red flags with my eyes closed.
I feel the dedication as you sculpt manipulations,
Careful where you place your mind games.
Your actions will come back to haunt you one day,
And the thought is entertaining,
Because you're not the first,
And although it's draining,
You won't be the last.
But you will prove that I do learn from the past,
As the insecurities you hide burn through your words,
My refusal to yield cuts deep,
Your need for control grows steep,

And that's not a mountain I'm willing to die on.

hard

Expression and emotionless,
I deal with emotions less.
Exhaled them in savasana,
They bring nothing but strong desires to show and prove,
Hiding in numbness keeps me sane.
Piling on any and everything to busy my brain,
I love to forget I have a heart.
I have no need to leave from behind my safety,
And you're not slick enough to maneuver through the lasers,
It's impossible to evade the alarms with your charm,
No one is capable of getting inside.
Shattered glass remains scattered from the last time,
I have too much to lose,
And you'll bring nothing but too much to hide,

I'm not fine.
And I never will be if I open up again,
I'm protective and defensive,
My softness is out of commission,
Please abort this mission.

sis is tired,
sis is me

Tired of ending love before it begins,

(But grateful for the ability to see the proper end).

Tired of breaking up with potential I never agreed to be with,

When is graduation from this lesson?

Praying for and aligning with what I hope to attract,

But what's the point if anyone can weasel through that?

How many more losses are needed?

I feel like I've learned.

Are we sure these selections are what I deserve?

How many more before my angels appear on the date,

Point at my company's face and say *"this is the one you've earned"*?

If I spot another red flag I'm slapping somebody's
mama with it,
Stop trying to join my peace while bringing noth-
ing beneficial to it,
Go heal.
Leave me alone.

distance makes
the heart lack
fondness

I may be projecting but this is upsetting.

Paranoia sitting on my heart,

Verify the intentions you've held from the start.

Who's banking on who to be there when needed?

Who's the one to choose if this is real or just convenient?

When it rested in your hands you slowly handed it back,

When cracks formed in what was had, you opted to make it last,

But what we have left is barely intact.

Not nearly what it was, still cherished but there's no necessity in what it's become.

Don't give the chance to create more distance in
the distance,
Don't let up on efforts because you've physically
gone missing,
Yet assume feelings will still glisten.
I wanted so much what was snatched away,
Maybe if it was meant to be you would've stayed.

lose, lose

You ask something great of me,
Something I wish I could deliver,
Something I wish you could reciprocate.
A request bathed in sweet memories and skin radiating steam,
Dancing shadows climbing walls with street lights peeking through cracked blinds.
A request spoken aloud that's much harder than it seems, and only feasible in dreams:

Just stay. Just remain in this place that is ours, shared and confirmed and redeemed as sacred as we make it, you've always been welcome.

You've always been welcome to be all you say.
I wish your heart believed in your tongue,
I wish my mind would believe in the power of love and its ability to change even someone like you,
To influence you to do all you say you would like to.

I wish I was a wishful thinker.

So I could live in the ignorant bliss required to deliver such desires, snuggling deep into potential, unlocking chance after chance, losing more and more of who I am with big hopes of winning a reality that matches my fantasy, my spirit is destined to die in the meantime, I'll become merely a shell.

So the choice lies between two fireless hells:
One in which I stay immersed within a beautiful lie,
Or one in which I go on forever frozen inside.

unbothered

Don't think I'm lying when I say I don't care,
You're no prize and this is no game,
You can act all you want.
Your charades pretending to be unphased are amusing,
It's confusing as you reject the suggestion to go our separate ways.
But anyway,
Whatever this is, it is no longer.
It came and left and you came and left empty-handed,
There's no turning back,
No trying to recoup your losses,
No trying to regain power,
I still have all of me and want no more of you.
Want to cut all ties, we're not tight any longer,
There may have been something there but it's not any longer.

If any part of me did care,
You'd still only see me unbothered.

everywhere
you go...

I can find the time to lie about my feelings,
A spotless mind to take the pain away,
I can take what's mine and go about my dealings,
But it's bound to come back on another day,
I can go, I can go free
To the end of the sea,
To the end of the world,
But it will find me
I can go, I can go free
To the west of the west,
To the east of the east,
But it will find me

left behind

Where have you been?

Arms should be tired from flying to new heights, feet sore from great strides,

Eyes set to blink twice by the sight of unfamiliar places in the space you created between us.

That's all that could explain it.

You've been busy discovering so no time for re-covering that thing we buried.

That thing we put on hold.

Maybe I should've followed suit,

Instead of solely watching the seconds evolve to minutes evolve to hours and floating numbers amidst my brain counting the days.

Because now you're back, but you're not you any-more and I'm still the same.

You tried to speak without words but I wasn't fit to listen.

Tried to warn me you're on a journey and I assumed I could come with you,

But the qualifications went unspoken too.

Only the truly qualified could notice what it would take.

You could've never taken me,

I wasn't ready.

And after all those seconds, minutes, hours and days I didn't notice a thing until you stood back before my face.

Right here, right now...

It goes without saying...

I know this time.

I know I should've evolved with the time.

I know I should've done more than wait.

There's a reason why you're always so quick to go, you constantly need to reach and extend, satisfaction is never yours, those standards are never met and it shows.

And my contentment is ever-present, I'm just happy to breathe, happy to experience your presence, my vision is immersed in a tunnel of you, why think about growth?

Why think about me at a time like this?

My soul wide and shut, vessel sleepless as my imagination tracks you. Thanks to the silence that I couldn't read, the language of your eyes I was unable to interpret, I thought you were lost but it's actually been me,

I didn't know.

But now I do.

You've been everywhere but here, hoping by the time you circled back I would understand, and when you decided to close the space and reappear I would have outgrown who I am,

But I didn't know the plan.

The little bit I was late will cost me,

It already has.

I'll never be able to keep up with you.

survive the night

The sun leaves and I can't trust myself,
The reasons aren't as clear,
This season is testing my will,
These summer nights aren't the same.
Salty cheeks replace salty ocean air at silent hours,
Sleep replaced with endless replays,
Trying to remember the meaning behind these self-inflicted delays,
My pillow whispers,
"Just survive the night.
The sun will return,
The darkness will release you,
The light will distract your mind from what's missing,
You'll be too busy to hear the loneliness.
Too focused on starting the day to obsess over the endings,

And why leaving them alone to be alone is best fitting,
Just survive the night."

RIP

Tired of crying over failed fantasies,
The lover needs a lifetime.
Wondering why I'm always everything needed,
But never found at the right time.
Why I'm forced to step back and wonder,
Why the greatest possibilities never align.
Why I'm forced to constantly play the one that
got away,
Why the space is never safe enough for me to stay.
The weight of the love I wish to give away,
Makes my heart ache.
Tired of crying over failed fantasies,
But never tired of handing my heart to faith.
Placing dream scenarios on a pedestal,
Believing reality will see the day.
Believing the perfection meant for me is on its way,
And I'll find sincerity in its flaws.
Remaining receptive to the softest fall,

But the strength of my faith doesn't blind me to it all.

There's nowhere for red flags to hide nor the warning signs,

The lessons from the past don't allow me to be blind.

My hope does not equate to naivete,

I clearly see the difference between something to work through and being played.

I see the difference between what's displayed and attempted to be portrayed,

So, here another fantasy is laid.

lies

I'm a liar.
My mind plays tricks on me,
And I'm starting to lose sight,
Of what's fake and what's real.
It says I'm not worthy of what I want,
I don't do enough, I'm not enough,
I don't deserve the nice things, I can't afford them,
I can't afford to do too much,
Why them and not me?
Because they're them and I'm me.
Failure consumes,
I talk myself out of visions before they can even
pretend to manifest,
I hardly put up a fight,
I constantly give into fear.
I say I keep every promise to myself
Because it sounds good,
I say I always do what I say I'm going to do,

But I only trust myself enough to exceed others'
expectations,
    When mine are on the line I rarely come through.
    No wonder people hate to be alone.
    You can't run from yourself forever,
    You can't disguise the fake forever,
    You can't avoid the truth forever.
    And the upside is this is as low as I can get,
    I'm ready to climb and becoming one with the
truth is the first step.

lost

Where did you go?
My inquiring mind needs to know.
Will you come back to me soon?
There's no one quite like you.
Do you know what you did to me?
Elusive and hypnotizing,
You once took me to new heights,
Once provided a perspective of magic,
I loved to see the world through your actions and habits.
You set me free and locked me in at the same time,
Showed me gratitude and drive then suddenly stepped aside,
I have yet to find you since.
I look in the mirror and see someone I don't recognize,
I've been looking for you ever since,

I didn't know it was possible to lose you until I lost you.

I didn't know how much I needed you until I lost you.

unfelt

Lately I've been feeling empty,
And it's written all over my face.
The air we share isn't the same,
Heart rate settled,
Desire's burn is tame,
I would like so much to care.
To feel open and present instead of just there.
Blank and shivering from stares well below freez-
ing,
Waiting for something to shake,
When something should've long ago claimed the
space,
If it was actually meant to take place.
No forcing blood to rush, minds to brighten from
enlightenment, exposed teeth from excitement, this
potential has no hands or feet there's no ability to
leap and no chance to reach and no way to grasp
what it needs.

No way to fill me,
No way for you to feel me.

apart

The voice wading in the banks of your memory no longer belongs to me.

Riding where the wind blows, growing out the shadows,

The past beneath my feet influences the sky's movements,

You know one of many past lives well.

The voice calling hair on your arms to stand,

A future buried in the sand haunts visions once had,

We can't all grow as planned.

A shared history split by an inevitable forecast.

fresh out of
benefit of the
doubt

They always know what they did,
Always know what they're doing,
Always know what they plan to do and not do.
Do you give the benefit of the doubt because they
deserve it,
Or because you need the excuse to be true?
Save yourself,
By accepting they're just as aware as anyone else.

IN MOTION II

dreams tell me things

Some summer days give frostbite,
I should have blinked twice.
Sometimes I see it how I want it,
And don't believe what it is.
Dressing for desire and not reality,
The misunderstandings don't register to me,
The clouds love to follow me,
I must be doing something wrong.
My first instincts blame me,
I made myself my worst enemy,
I need to re-evaluate.
Blinked back to consciousness before it was too
late,
I don't need to control it,
Just ebb and flow with it,
And it feels good to finally smile.

It feels good to see the sun,
I haven't seen it in a while.

only promise

Not much of a time waster,
It's either there or it's not.
No jumping at possibilities and potential,
Only promise.
True interest has no questions,
Its sincerity glows.
When absence bears confusion,
Let it go.
If it doesn't scream positivity,
If it isn't overwhelming and caring,
Delighted and daring,
Calm and a little scary,
It's not a thing.

the standard

I know what I seek is complex and elusive,
Inspired by wishful thinking and an overactive imagination,
I give perfection several qualities
And refuse to believe it can't all be mine.
My entire being burns to reciprocate my requests,
I'm pressed.
And with every new level reached,
The search grows steeper,
I crave something deeper,
But I'll raise my standards higher before I regress,
I'll wait forever for my equal before I settle for less,
I can't make the same mistakes and still hope for the best.
I can't go against what I need just to feel anything,
It's never worth it,
My value doesn't deserve it.

affirm

No need to ask for more when you've asked for it all.
Claimed.
Feel the details of what you name,
Lie in the cracks and creases,
Dive deep into the vision.
Something greater than this world is duly committed,
To nurturing you and watching you,
Bloom.
Feel the passion,
The purpose deep in your soul's mission,
As the architect, the dreamer, the innovator, believer, artist, and redeemer,
Your inspiration aspires to revive the dead inside,
You are meant to live in a masterpiece.
You are meant to be a master of peace,
Settling for nothing but the highest quality hues,

Settling for nothing but the utmost confidence in you,

To place what's in your heart in clear view to see it through.

There's nothing that can block you from destiny,

No situation or circumstance,

How much or little you're given or believed in,

How much or little you're tested won't change the plan.

Think higher before you think again,

Stay faithful to the win,

Stay faithful to what you wish to gain,

And know a way is guaranteed to be made.

Because you fucking claimed it.

10/10/2020

My favorite of life's filters,
Citrus and tulips deepen to royalty,
Today's reign fades with its illusions.
The future approaches and time pushes our feet,
No matter how you go,
You will go.
Be cognizant of how you paint the world as you
grow.

meet me there

It's already happening,
I just have to meet me there.
A recurring vision that keeps me consistent,
On an end of the Earth I hope to be immersed in,
Where clouds graze the ocean of all our dreams.
Breeding inspiration from playing with words,
Held by a love as deep as the endless view,
And dreamy eyes hold my heart outside my body,
With a smile that beams through to my soul.
Living what I've always lived for,
Because I sacrificed what I wanted,
For what I wanted more,
And stayed forever loyal to what I needed,
To look back and say I finally succeeded,
I see it.

views

I'm surrounded by angels with homes of different heights,
And hearts with different angles,
Casting light within me,
For the discovery of a layer I've yet to find.
Gifts of lessons or pure devotion,
Hiding in plain sight with unclear motives,
My eyes now see,
How easily they can lie.
Unlocking the sight of a half-full glass,
Finding the shine in the darkest corners of life,
Reading everything as close as possible to minds,
Staying safe by remaining in between the lines.

loner

Sometimes, I need to be left the fuck alone.
There lies a brand of peace within my solitude
I can't afford to lose,
Don't make it about you.
Sometimes, I don't want anyone to share my air,
To fill the silence,
To feel me.
Sometimes, I just need to hear me.
Sometimes, I need to part ways from everyone else
To re-connect with and re-evaluate myself,
I'm one of those.
A self-proclaimed loner,
An introvert with an internal timer,
I could love you to the end of this world
And still need my space.
Don't make it about you,
Don't force me to choose.
Don't make it me against you,

Because you will always lose.

smell the roses

I can feel in my spirit what's real,

And whatever is artificial is no big deal.

I don't need anyone that doesn't stop and feel the sun,

Doesn't stop and see the stars,

Doesn't acknowledge the breeze and their ability to breathe.

If we float along the clouds, will you stop and look down?

Or rest your head in the sky and get lost in being found?

everything you touch

What I desire always arrives on time and in abundance,

There's gold in the air and at my fingertips.

Always working in mysterious ways with the most high,

An alchemist alchemizing,

And giving limits no life,

They don't exist here.

Avoiding language based in fear,

Can't be a part of certain conversations,

When you know your words are powerful.

Unmoved by certain moves,

Can't be a part of certain rooms,

When you know your presence is powerful.

When your energy is bright you attract what aligns,

But you also attract anything addicted to light.
Go where your essence is guided,
And loving energy is stated,
And everything you touch can remain sacred.

just want to live

I don't care to be loved by you.
You can have nothing to do with me.
I just want to go for runs, feed my melanin rays
from the sun,
Rest in my home, be left alone,
Provide and hold peace,
Reconnect, and breathe.
You can feel whatever you wanna feel.
Hatred when I cross your eye,
Despise my culture, my face, my voice, my life.
Allow that soul-sucking evil to contaminate your
insides,
Excuse yourself from spaces in which I reside,
I promise I pay you no mind,
That's your issue not mine.
I'll never ask for a crumb of sympathy you could
spare,
Nor compassion, nor signs of knowledge,

I know the awareness is really there.

Awareness of what *'Black lives matter'* signifies and means,

You just choose to shift and skew,

To acknowledge would force admitting that you simply do not agree.

I don't care to direct my endangered breath toward brick walls,

Begging for something to give.

I care about actions, whatever they may be,

Whether working behind the scenes or out in these streets,

I care about our voices, our stories, our perspectives,

I care about my people, I do my part for my people.

I just want us to live.

timelines

The old me wants a comeback,
And I simply can't afford that.
You know how easy it would be to just let her be?
To let her reclaim her place and lead the way,
And vow to conquer anything or body in her way,
But it wouldn't be the same.
She wouldn't even survive in this timeline,
She doesn't know the way.
We traveled lightyears and she saw the value to disappear,
She doesn't truly know what it's like here.
On the other side of all that space and all that time,
This new life,
It tastes different.
And while it's harder to maintain,
A new me I just met,
And navigating a new lane,
It would have been easier to stay the same,

But she was released for a reason,
We agreed to change.
And while this space can be cold,
What must be done must be done alone,
Who we've become must grow quicker and much
stronger,
Than who we are no longer.
Although she's been living longer,
She has to stay where we left her.
We have to let old feelings fall from the ceiling,
And vivid dreams pull us into memories,
To remember why we left,
To remember why we leapt.

known unknowns

A different world behind an attainable threshold,
It has always seemed so far,
Until clouds seeped through and circled the hills,
That encompasses who we are.
And it can all change with the seasons,
The concept of time suddenly so meaningless,
A hole in our minds sewn by our life plan's seam-
stress.
The visions let me have my lie,
They already knew what was destined.
The eyes didn't need to see it for it to be it.

impenetrable

There is nothing you can say
To ever make me feel a way,
Funny of you to assume such power.
The past may be littered with reactions,
Of losing myself in people like you,
But sometimes we get sick of our own shit.
And rebirth begins,
With a lesson in self-respect,
Taught by our own reflection.
We learn to grow new skin,
And give the world no choice but to leave us alone,
Or get to know us again.
And we remain unmoved by either decision,
Remain detached from every opinion,
Protected by impenetrable self-love.
Your ego runs deep,
But it stops here.

new life

I'll never go back to suppressing me,
I need me.
This one life won't be made artificial,
I'm not here for pretending,
I've tasted freedom,
And I'll never complain,
About the amount on my plate,
That it takes to obtain.
No safety net,
No plan B,
Just my greatest asset smoking liabilities,
Tell my old life it will never see me again.

home

Everything can change and yet, remain the same.
Revisiting a release bred by my wishing,
My hoping, my dreaming to one day get away.
Leaving for something I wasn't sure existed,
I go and lie elated in the ability to flee,
To be recreated, renewed, and released,
And return to recharge with what lacks in re-inventing,
Reminded of what sparked the obsession for change,
And the love running through my veins.
The source of the most meaningful accolades,
You made me, you raised me, you paved my way.
The consistency I run from and simultaneously crave,
Everything to me without being my everything,
Meaning the world without being the world,
Exactly what's been missing,

And the motivation to go missing.

reminder (11/11/ 2020)

I don't ask to be saved or retrieved,

I see what I need and conquer.

I am always who I need to be when I need to be her,

And what is attracted in each phase or facet,

Is a reflection of the value placed in each sought asset.

I reshape as seen fit, my foundation strengthens each shift.

No sunken energies could ever deprive me.

I don't match, I exceed.

I don't attach, I proceed.

I take what is given and protect my mind,

My heart learned not to beat for potential.

Sometimes I slide off track but I always come back.

Sometimes I slack but I never lack.

Sometimes I need reminders and this is that.

INSANE

cold

A sociopath receives her karma.

I'm not easily moved. I tend to stand firm. So, I fall for nothing.

There is no belief in love and no interest in what comes with chasing its dream. I don't wish to be powerless, dependent, ignorant. The falsity of passion and trust raises the parts within us meant to remain buried. Not everything deserves the sun.

I hardly believe in friendship, but I do believe in utility. I have no family. And no one deemed worthy enough to come into my space and be used by me. She is the first. She gives a second presence when my own isn't enough. Someone to watch my back when conquering the city nights and share a laugh.

We do what best girlfriends do, and she has someone she can rely on to be there for her. Because for her to be there for me, I have to reciprocate, and I do well at protecting her from anyone who doesn't mean well. They'll only distract her and get in the way of the utility I receive from our perceived friendship.

Her eyes follow the horchata as it travels up the straw and into her mouth. I look out the wide windows of the restaurant and watch families play on the ocean's hairline.

She could at least crack a smile after the effort I've made. She's been in the darkness of her apartment for two weeks, breathing stale air and mourning a love that was pronounced dead long before his heart stopped beating. I wish she would save her world the suffering, revolving it around something so trivial as the death of a body that housed a soul who didn't truly care about her.

She wasn't strong enough to leave on her own and she should have been. If she were, this burden wouldn't be nearly as heavy.

His journey to hell wouldn't have come so soon.

If I could empathize with her I still wouldn't. I know the full story. Sympathy won't even try to activate. I just want things back to normal, which is the purpose of today. To bring her out of the darkness to her favorite restaurant by the beach. To help her get up and move on. Hold up my end of the exchange. Which is why I sent her back upstairs when she came out to the car in the same sweats and hoodie she'd been wearing since the night of the funeral. She should have known I would make her change. Just like she knew to try and cover her swollen eyelids with strip eyelashes and the red marks of tension on her face from wiping tears with her summer foundation. We're nearing winter.

It's not perfect, but it's a start. I force a smirk at her efforts.

"The police called me in for questioning again," she says through her teeth, the straw still a bridge between her mouth and the glass. "They seem suspicious of me."

I spot the waiter approaching with our food. "There's nothing to worry about."

She bites into her favorite fish tacos and my tortilla chip snaps in the lukewarm queso.

They constantly argued. She would vent to me about his issues he took out on her, then return to him every time. I was elated when she traveled to the opposite end of the fourth floor and showed up at my door late one night with glistening cheeks and a shirt wet and reeking of whiskey. He went off on her again with slurred words and insecure scenarios, throwing his drink at her before putting her out and falling asleep to the sound of her banging on the door. He plays this game and she always loses, but he usually lets her back inside after a while. This time was different. It was proof it would only continue to get worse. Their neighbors peered through peepholes and one was bold enough to open their door and complain about the noise, forcing her to quit attempting to get back inside and come to me.

I thought they were finally done and this mess of a ride was through after that. But she went back down the hall the next day. I gave her my spare key and let her know to use it *only* when they are really done and she needs somewhere to go. She never did. She stayed. Things never changed.

"I knew that was you!"

A face I may have seen before stops at our table.

They exchange pleasantries and she swallows the food in her mouth just as the face fixes its own mouth to dig. "How are you holding up?"

I remember who this is now. A friend of the ex. Someone who tried clinging to her because she was dating him, and I saw straight through the artificial air of kindness. She didn't mean well. People rarely do.

"I'm alright, I guess. First time leaving the house in a while," she looks at me. *To* me. She knows my thoughts about this woman.

"Well, thank goodness for friends," the face smiles at me. I stare at it. She leans in closer to her. " If you need anything I'm a phone call away... I can't imagine what you're going through. He was a great guy, I'm really going to miss him too." The face stares through her with a head tilted in questionable compassion and forced concern.

"I found my boyfriend on the kitchen floor with foam running from his mouth. That image has been playing over and over in my mind for the past two weeks and I'm just trying to replace it with my favorite fish tacos at my favorite restaurant by my favorite beach for at least a couple hours. Yet, here you are reminding me how incredibly sad my life is."

The face blinks and looks between us. "I didn't mean any harm. He was my friend, and I'm genuinely concerned about you."

A tear falls onto the plate. The face kneels down to hug her but I stand and shove her back. "I think you should go."

The face leaves.

I pretend I know what to do when someone cries, moving the stray hair from her face and handing her a napkin but the damage has been done. "I want to go. Now."

I wish she would have let me get to-go boxes for the tacos as I drive us back inland. She leans against the window, occasionally sniffling. Occasionally wiping her face. The end of her sleeve is stained brown, the strip eyelashes are stuffed in her pocket, and her day out of the darkness is ruined.

"It's not your fault," I try to reassure her but I know it falls on deaf ears. She says nothing.

I gave her the best advice I could at the time and we both did the best we could with the plan we came up with. I deleted the Google searches.

"You have nothing to worry about," I say into the void of silence within the car, half to her and half to myself.

Her weighted voice surprises me. "Nothing will ever be the same."

"Did you do everything I told you to?"

"Yes."

We both did everything we could and everything we were supposed to. We will be okay. We will move on from this. And it'll be better because he's no longer in the picture. She can be there for me whenever I need her with no distractions or worries. I'm the closest thing to a friend she's got. She should be thanking me for all I've done for her.

Every time I arrive at our building, I anticipate flashing lights and cold metal suffocating my wrists. I park and we ride the elevator in silence. She steps onto our floor first and heads toward her apartment and I head in the opposite direction toward mine. She rounds her corner and I round mine. When I go to unlock my door, I realize it is already unlocked.

I wait for a moment. I listen. If someone is on the other side of this door waiting for me, they already know I'm here. I imagine my studio crammed with uniforms and large guns. I wonder if I left my weed on the coffee table. I open the door.

Weed is still on the coffee table. Clothes on the floor. Window by my bed still cracked open and the curtains blow in the breeze. The kitchen looks the same. No one is in the bathroom.

Robbers, maybe?

My TV is still here, my laptop is still plugged into the charger, my money stash is still under the dracaena.

This entire situation is getting to my head. I must have forgotten to lock the door when I left. I have become one with stress over something that has nothing to do with me. Maybe I was better off alone. Maybe I don't need the utility she has served me, the company she brings when I could use someone to breathe beside, the body to lean on stumbling drunk out of our favorite bar, I was just fine by myself. But she needs me right now. I compose a text message.

Everything is okay. You did the right thing. Maybe we can go to our favorite bar tomorrow?

I press send and look up and that's when I see it. The closet door is closed. I always leave it open.

I turn a vase upside down and shake the plastic flowers to the floor, then hold the glass tightly as I place one foot in front of the other. I listen, but I hear nothing. I want to pray but I can't. I swing open the closet door ready to shatter the glass against whoever appears in front of me and there is nothing. I push the hangers of clothes to the side only to reveal the wall behind them. Nothing. But a pair of shoes I rarely wear are slightly out of place, one of them now on top of a pair of shoes I wear regularly.

I pick them up and they look the same. Just not the way I left them. I drop the vase and turn them upside down, and something falls out.

A small plastic baggie lies at my feet. I pick it up and it is tied in a knot. The plastic is clouded with some type of powder. I try to peer through it and it looks like marbles are inside. No... mints. No... pills?

Wait.

My eyes are called to the top of the dresser a few

steps away and the spare key rests on top of it. My phone vibrates.

This is all your fault. I'm sorry it's come to this.

A banging at the door, an announcement, and a large bang knocking the door off the hinges. My studio is flooded with uniforms and orders. I wonder how sorry she really is as I bring my hands behind my head. I think about how well she told the story to the familiar face as mine is pressed into the carpet. I regret the utility and question how long she'd been planning to pin this on me as more boots enter my view from the floor. I just had the idea. I just did the Google search. This is what I get for helping someone. The cold metal suffocates my wrists, and I can't help but smile as I realize she truly *only* used the key after they were really done.

richa$$ness

A future-based story of a scorned scientist that takes work home with her.

Merci yawns as she taps the screen on the coffeemaker. **Dark Roast. (1) Cream. (2) Sugars.**

She closes her eyes and listens as the machine growls and the scent of energy fills her nostrils. Her satin robe untied and hanging off her shoulders, she jumps when she feels his hands sliding the fabric in place from behind her.

"Stop sneaking up on me like that," she turns and smiles.

He plants a kiss on her forehead then looks behind her, grabbing the now filled mug and handing it to her before placing his travel mug and tapping his caffeinated order in. Dark Roast. (1) Cream. (2) Sugars.

"I like to see you jump," he smiles. The machine growls again and she watches as he leans against the opposite counter. His suit tailored to perfection, one ankle crossed over the other as he squeezes in a few seconds of frowning at work emails on his phone. "What do you have planned today?" he asks without looking up from the screen.

Merci turns back around as the last drop of coffee spits into the travel mug. The machine's hand places the top and screws it on, then extends the platform on which the mug sits. She grabs it and glides her slippers across the floor toward him. "Manicure, take the dogs to the groomers, and maybe wash my truck. It got a little dusty when we were out of town."

He finally looks up from his phone and grabs the mug. "You should set up the automatic washes."

"You're right, I should."

"It's in the settings on the dashboard."

She smiles. "Thank you, I'll do it today."

He gestures to the mug in his hand. "And thank you. So, those plans cover about an hour of your day. What about the rest?"

They laugh and he kisses her forehead before heading to the door.

"I'll figure something out," she says. "Are you working late tonight?"

"I hope not. I miss you already," he looks over his shoulder and winks. "I'll keep you posted. Maybe we'll have dinner at that new restaurant we were talking about the other day. They're doing a soft opening, I'll have a colleague get us on the list."

"That sounds perfect," Merci answers, watching her husband disappear out the door, and listening as the garage door opens, then the engine of his sports car revs.

***

She arrives at the front door of the groomers, the two yorkies playing around her sleek black sneakers as she carefully places her face in front of the scanner. The green lines analyze her identity then the door unlocks. **Membership Confirmed. (1) delivery.**

The inside of the groomers is empty, and the dogs wait for her to remove their leashes. The walls are lined with six large compartments with ramps leading up to their rounded entrances. Once she unhooks them, they both take off to their own compartments and run inside.

Tails wag as she heads to one, presses a couple buttons causing the door to close and machine to start, then she repeats with the other. While the robots do their jobs, she heads to the delivery station. A few more buttons to press, then a message appears on the screen. **Stand back. Locker 8 Opening.**

Locker 8 pops open and Merci peers inside to find a single red rose and a note. *Not working late. Reservations at 7. Love, Yours.* She sniffs the rose and smiles, then three rings go off inside of her ears.

"I'll be over once I finish these errands," she says aloud.

Three more rings. "Okay, I'll come by straight from here."

Two rings.

Sixty seconds later, both compartments open and the yorkies run down the ramps with fresh haircuts, bows, and clipped nails. Merci hooks their leashes back on and they exit the establishment.

***

The SUV self-drives up tight, winding roads of the city's prestigious hills.

Merci stares out the window, mindlessly petting the pups and spotting the hidden view of the ocean that only appears between each home they pass. The SUV finally slows and pulls into the driveway of their destination, stopping beside a luxury SUV identical to hers but much cleaner.

She taps through the settings on the dashboard to set up the automatic washes per her husband's suggestion, but the front door of the home opens and a woman steps outside causing the dogs to go crazy. They bark and jump against the doors, urging Merci to let them out so she quickly initiates one wash and gets out the SUV just in time for it to begin spraying itself with water and oozing suds.

Merci lets go of the leashes, allowing the dogs to run ahead and the woman kneels down as they greet her with excitement larger than their bodies.

"About time you got here," the woman stands. The dogs run inside the home and the ladies follow.

"I came as soon as I could," Merci watches the woman close the front door, then stand before her. The marble floors of the foyer shine under their shoes and a crystal chandelier the size of a small car sparkles above their heads.

The woman eyes Merci, grabbing her hand and spinning her around. "What is with these all black outfits?"

"He's been really into black lately. He requests it all the time."

The woman sucks her teeth. "That basic motherfucker." She heads further into the home and Merci follows behind her yellow blazer dress and yellow heels like a shadow. They emerge into the kitchen and the open wall facing the back of the home paints a clear view of the ocean spanning to the horizon. The swimming pool ripples in the breeze and the dogs play in the sunlight.

"Do you need anything?" the woman asks.
"A few adjustments."

Merci watches as a machine pours white wine into two glasses then extends each of them forward to be collected. They rhythmically tap their glasses together then step out to the patio to begin their weekly meeting.

"I want to add more color to your wardrobe preferences. If he wants black, give him the brightest colors ever. Something big enough to entertain me with his dissatisfaction but small enough to not become an issue. Wear bright red at dinner tonight," the woman chuckles.

Merci sips her wine. "Okay. I would also like more sympathy. There was an awkward moment in Santorini with his friends. He told me later I should 'read the room'. I could tell he may have been embarrassed by me, but he tried to laugh it off after some time. I think it'd be beneficial to everyone if situations like that don't happen again."
The woman laughs. "Honey, I saw exactly what happened and respectfully, it was hilarious. Poor Tanya was crying about her cheating husband and you tried to console her by saying at least someone else is sucking his-,"

"She tells us all the time how she hates doing it!" Merci cringes. "I thought it was a positive outlook and would make her feel better."

The woman laughs harder. "I don't think your sympathy needs adjusting, maybe your humor is just set too high." She walks into the kitchen to grab her phone off the counter and quickly taps the screen. "Okay, we got wardrobe, humor, anything else? I would love to give you more sass to combat his condescension. When he mansplained how to turn on the auto-wash for the truck I nearly vomited."

"Do you think I should be more sassy with him?" Merci asks.

The woman considers her question briefly, then rolls her eyes. "Ugh, probably not. Defeats the whole purpose if we take the antics too far."

Merci nods.

"I'll boost your confidence a little instead. He definitely loves the more quiet, gentle energy but I think he would find it sexy if you got just a little bold every once in a while."

The woman approaches Merci and raises the back of her shirt. She taps a few more times on her phone and four rings go off in Merci's ears. Merci feels the rush up her back and the woman watches as the green orbs underneath her skin glow from her lower back to the base of her neck then disappear. Merci's head feels light for a few seconds before returning back to normal and the woman lowers her shirt.

"Alright, you're all set," the woman says, returning her phone to the counter and taking another sip of her wine. She kneels down, catching the dogs attention so they run back toward her. "I miss them so much."

Merci watches as she pets the fur babies. "Why don't you buy new ones? To keep here with you?"

The woman pretends to be offended. "Girl, these are my babies. I can't just replace them," she downs the remaining wine in the glass and continues to pet the dogs, shaking her head. "He really did me so wrong. You would think I'd be over it by now. I clearly have won. But, I don't know, something just keeps me bothered by his audacity. The way he could turn on me the way he did."

Merci remains quiet. She knows the woman just needs to vent.

"He thought he left me with nothing. He took away my friends, my home, my life. He could have at least let me take my dogs. You know the judge was Tanya's cheating husband's father?"

"Yeah," Merci shakes her head. "It's insane."

The woman stands and faces Merci. "Insane. And he is so much more thoughtful and kind to you. So patient and courteous. Like yeah, he's still a particular asshole that needs everything to go his way or no way. He's a Virgo. But he really gives you a version of him I never knew existed. Spontaneous trips, dinner reservations, surprise roses at the groomers. All he showed me was how bad it could get, and all I did was help him become the successful man he is today."

"At least you have me," Merci says.

"Yeah. If your marriage wasn't the only thing allowing me to have everything I need, I would take you away from him in the most egregious and gut wrenching manner just to break him the way he broke me."

"Do what you must."

"Do you think I'm crazy?" the woman asks. "For creating you?"

"Absolutely not. I think you did what you needed to do. Do you think you're crazy?"

"I left my career because of him. Years of studies, lab testing, hours of interviews and months of trials to become a top scientist with a top secret agency. The security clearances, the highly confidential information, the discoveries we made. He never asked much about what I did for a living. As long as it put food on the table while he worked to build his company, and I dimmed my light to keep his fragile masculinity intact, he couldn't care less. Then his startup finally gets the funding and takes off like a rocket, and he urges me to stay home to focus on starting a family and to 'keep me soft'. When it turns out he also couldn't care less about having children, and just didn't want to have the only wife out of his business partners that didn't depend on their husbands to survive. He needed to feel needed and I gave him that because I was tired and being soft didn't sound too bad. Just for him to dump me when he was ready for something new. So no, I don't think I'm crazy. I think he lost sight of what type of woman I am after years of only seeing me play small for him."

Merci nods. "Exactly. Doing what you need to do."

"Doing what I do, period."

"Do you want your deposit now?"

"Hell yes!" The woman grabs her phone and taps the screen again.

Three more rings in Merci's ears. "Transfer amount $15,000 confirmed. Sending," she says.

"Even your 'weekly allowance' is more than what mine was," the woman scoffs as her phone chimes with receipt of the payment. "He would have a fit if he knew most of it was coming to me. And on top of the alimony? Ha!"

Merci laughs. "He would have a fit if he knew I was actually created in his ex-wife's secret laboratory built with his alimony payments, specifically designed to seduce and marry him and be a perfect, new version of her to get back at him and allow her to maintain the soft lifestyle she's grown to love and keep a relationship with her dogs he and his cheating friend's judge father wouldn't let her take in the divorce!"

The woman frowns. "Maybe I need to decrease your humor a little more. Why is it so dark?"

"It might be the stand-up comedy specials I've been watching."

"Your A.I brain is way too sensitive, Merci. Be careful with what you're consuming. I mean, it was kinda funny, but he was right, read the room, okay?"

"I'll work on that."

***

Merci watches as the woman pets the dogs goodbye. "See you next week?"

The woman stands and they hug each other. "You know it. Unless he takes you on another spontaneous trip to the Mediterranean Sea. And if so, I'll be watching," she waves her phone, the screen showing the view of herself from Merci's eyes.

Merci winks and the dogs follow close to her heels as she heads toward her freshly cleaned truck.

"I have to figure out a way to do your adjustments without you needing to be in the vicinity," the woman calls out.

"Why?" Merci stops and turns to face her.

"So you don't always need to stop by. You could send the deposits and receive adjustments from wherever, as long as the coast is clear."

"I'd still need to come over here, though," Merci says.

"Why?"

"So you can see your dogs."

The woman shakes her head. "See. Your sympathy levels are just fine. Your husband on the other hand...

maybe I can figure out a way to turn down his bitchassness."

maybe I can figure out a way to turn down his bitchassness."

familiar

A young woman signs up for an experiment that malfunctions.

I was intrigued by the possibility. And the thousand dollar payout for signing up. I needed new winter clothes and the tread on my tires was getting shameful.

What happens after we take our last breath has always been too beyond me to even attempt to fathom. I didn't prophesy or choose to believe in hopeful scenarios. If it was darkness, it was just darkness. If it was another realm, universe, life, whatever, then so be it. I preferred to live presently, and take every day I was given as it was received. But the day I went to sign the contract, I thought about death in a different way. I realized how much time I spent worried about the future or harping over the past, and with this realization, I was intrigued by the possibility of being able to experience all the small moments I may have missed one more time. I know now,

I would have backed out if I read the fine print. There had to have been something nestled in there regarding the probability of what would ultimately happen to me.

There's a lesson in here somewhere about money and curiosity leading me to my demise.

The night the experiment began wasn't soon after I opted in, but it was surely unexpected. It all moved so fast. Sometimes a scene would be recognized and simply chalked up to déjà vu. I re-loved the same and re-lost the same and re-learned every lesson. It all played out the way it had the first time around.

Then came the day that would never leave with its stained leaves and tied scarves and a gray tint covering the sky. I stood under the overcast and took a deep breath. A sense of discovery called me. I wondered how it knew my name and where to find me as my body answered. I knew the air was different that day. I knew the chill that struck my lower spine was attempting to pull me back into the safety of my home but I took it as a challenge. I walked and daydreamed about changing like the seasons and wished I could learn to let go like the leaves.

And I landed in a coffee shop.

Keyboards tapped with gusto and the smell of pumpkin spice reintroduced itself. I begged heat to form between the palms of my hands but still ordered something iced. Outside welcomed a smile as I returned to the sidewalk and collided with another body before I could take the first sip.

"I'm so sorry," she said as she kneeled down to pick up her fallen cellphone.
"No, that was me, I should have been more careful."

Her eyes let go of mine to travel south. The cold drink raced down the front of my jacket. My hand was soaked.

"Shoot, girl, I'll get you some napkins," she grabbed the cup and its displaced lid from my hand and a spiced breeze swept against my face as the entrance to the coffee shop closed behind her. I stood still as if any movement would increase the mess. People pretended not to stare as they walked by. I thought of how I shouldn't be here. I'd been standing in the same spot waiting for a stranger with coffee spilled on the front of my jacket for so long, anticipating how I would force my feet to take me home over and over. I imagined retiring to my couch and hanging up the call to discover the world today. Then I imagined her returning just to find me gone and I couldn't bring myself to do it. Then she finally emerged with napkins in one hand and another cup of something iced in the other.

First, I was awed by the ability of a stranger to be so friendly. Then, suspicion harbored in the pit of my stomach, analyzing her every move for signs of simply good acting.

I wiped my jacket and tossed the napkins in a nearby trash can. She handed me the fresh drink. "It's the least I could do. Pumpkin spice, right?" she laughed. "I could smell it. It's also my favorite order this time of year."

"Yeah," I smiled, suddenly noticing the strong scent emanating from my jacket. It's suddenly quite repulsive. "Thank you, you didn't have to do that."

She introduced herself and we walked along her life story. How she just moved here. No family on this coast. No friends yet. Just started back dating but it's been frustrating. Loves being alone but hates feeling alone. Hates starting over. Struggles with new people and their motives.

I listened to the loneliness in her voice and swam through a wave of information only someone desperate for connection would share so soon. I felt bad for her.

She told me about a guy she's interested in that invited her to a get-together this evening. "It may be far-fetched since we just met," she said. "But it'd be nice to have another woman with me. I don't want to go by myself, but I do want to go. I told myself I would get out more and this could be a start. Shit, inviting a person I just met off the street is a start too."

Her smile twitched. I knew what it was like to be nervous. Afraid of rejection, hopeful that taking a chance will result in the response you need and not the one that will make you regret stepping out of comfort.

This time around, the nerves on her lips read differently. She knew what to say for me to lower my guard and I took the bait. "Sure, I'll go with you."

***

I stared at my reflection in the dim lighting of my apartment. My favorite jeans. A plain t-shirt under a thrift store brown and tan plaid jacket. New combat boots I wasn't sure were appropriate for what I was about to walk into. I was tempted to call and ask if it would be more formal or casual, but I decided to trust myself for once.

She sent an address and the new tires on my car spun toward it. I'd rarely ever visited the area and only knew of certain restaurants I'd passed that night that I always wanted to try but never did. I noted them again, the fact I'd never get the chance still unbeknownst.

I parked on the street outside an apartment complex in which her location showed. One hand clutched the pepper spray inside my purse and the other pressed the lock button on my car's key fob several times, letting anyone in the vicinity know that my car's alarm was set. The sound of music grew less faint as I approached a building outside of which a group of smokers discussed a documentary passionately. Then I spotted her standing a few feet behind them. She waved me over then looked back down to her phone. Mine chimed with a message.

She's here. Coming inside.

"You haven't gone inside yet?" I asked.

Her furrowed brow urged me to show her the text I just received from her. I knew it wasn't for me. The first time, I figured it was for him. This time, I figured the same but the malice was potent.

She smiled and grabbed my arm. "Of course not. Not without you."

I followed her into the apartment. The only lighting in the living room was a red neon sign reading **No Regrets.** The kitchen light was bright but the bulb flickered. A man approached and she hugged him as she introduced us. He held out his hand and I hated the ring on his middle finger from first sight. A silver skull.

She poured us cups of tequila and orange juice and I felt eyes on me from the dark red of the living room. I felt out of place, but couldn't place why. I wondered if my boots were weird.

I missed my couch.

When she handed me my drink, I drowned my nerves. After two large gulps, the cup was nearly empty, but she filled it back to the brim. We joined the rest of the guests in the dark red and I opened up more. We talked and laughed and the music helped. She placed a hand on his knee and I looked out the window, studying the smokers standing in the same spot they were in when I arrived. My eyes focused onto one face of the group, so regular and indistinct. For a moment, it felt familiar. This space was familiar and it felt off and I felt like I should leave but I've felt this before in so many situations, each one seeming to have happened just yesterday with its details and my feelings and my misgivings being so clear. Every time I wanted to leave I would leave and I would worry about what I missed. This time I wanted to stay. It's harder trying to live with what could have been. And after the last drink she brought us back from the kitchen, it was harder for me to speak.

"Are you okay?" she frowned. "You're blinking a lot."

I tried not to blink and my eyes stung. "Yeah, I just haven't drank in a while."

"Let's go outside and get some air."

She grabbed my arm and our breath showed in the crisp night. First the chill relieved me then I felt uneasy. He and his skull ring followed behind us.

My head started pounding.

This night was becoming surreal. A meshing of scenes I'd seen before but while I breathed the familiar air a part of my mind held constant to the belief that it was just the mystery of deja vu.

Her voice faded away. "I'll grab you some water."

No. I knew what came after this. I knew what this was. But I wasn't me. Reliving came with the same emotions and feelings and truly being immersed in every experience of my life, but I was just looking through a glass. I had no control. I couldn't change a thing. I didn't think it would include this part at all, let alone repeatedly. I should have read the fine print. It was a new experiment after all.

The first time around, I should have pressed her to stay with me. It may not have changed much, but I could have tried. I should have trusted my first mind.

She disappeared into the apartment and he tried to lighten the mood. It worked the first time. This time, I wanted to cry through my ignorant drunken smile. I didn't want to burden them. I hated how childish I felt, unable to hold my liquor around people I hardly knew. That part of me looked at the door of the apartment and waited for her to return while the silenced part of me knew she wasn't coming back. Maybe she was in on it. Or maybe someone inside got to her too. Perhaps the answers would have come, had I not signed away the chance to know what really lies beyond life.

"I'm gonna go to my car and call someone to come get me," I heard my words clearly but he looked confused.

He let me walk away. He let me believe I would get to my car safely. I reached for the key fob and looked through my purse for the green case of my phone. I struggled to tap my thumb against the brightness of the screen. Then I remembered being a woman out in the middle of the night alone and not sober and dug into the bag for my pepper spray. I reached the curb my car was parked beside and tripped over it. That's when someone grabbed my arm.

I looked back as I struggled to regain my balance, ready to press down on the pepper spray but it was him and his familiar face. "I couldn't let you walk off alone."

I hesitated. He seemed genuine. I was awed by the ability of a stranger to be so friendly. Then he snatched the pepper spray out of my hand and the green case of my phone hit the concrete. He picked me up and my boots no longer touched the ground and the skull pinched my lips as his hand pressed my fear inside and the fear intensified. I sounded the alarm on my car and he snatched the key fob out my hand before dropping me to the ground. I barely saw him raise his fist, but I focused on the cool Autumn air every time it struck. My eyes closed for the last time. The last moments of the last night of my life happened in darkness. I didn't want to see. I don't even know if he meant to do what he did to me, I don't know if taking my life was part of the plan, I don't know what they really wanted from me. I just wish I'd read the fine print.

I was intrigued by the payment and the possibility of reliving my life. Now I contemplate the concept of no regrets as the same gray tint returns again and again. A mistake I signed up to make. Now I'll never quit wishing I followed my first mind.

nightmares

A young woman must overcome her shadows to save her life.

She finds it hard to see the good in many things. She squints and racks her brain for the silver linings, but reality remains gray. It hasn't always been like this.

Chloe used to see the glitter. Opportunities that formed stars in her eyes, she believed she would put in the work and climb the ladder, and what awaited her at the top was notoriety for claiming space as a Black woman in this society. Things have changed.

And right now, she's held captive by a blank stare. The busy sounds of rushing waiters passing between tables and clanging utensils against dishes muffle in the background. Until Drea snaps her back to the gray.

"Girl, come on, grab your shot!" the birthday girl orders.

Chloe blinks to find all of her friends' eyes impatiently waiting for her to grab the ounce of hell that has appeared in front of her and join the celebration. "Oh, no," she shakes her head. "Drea, you take mine. It's your birthday and I'm not drinking."

She slides the glass into Drea's orbit but it bounces back.

Her friends are everything. They save her more than endanger her, but nights like these lead to the latter. She doesn't blame them. We all tend to be caught up in ourselves, sometimes it's tough to remember how much someone hates something, especially something as common within their friend group as drinking. Especially when it only takes one rebuttal to her refusal for her to cave in. Chloe's boundaries reflect this chapter of her life, somewhere between trying to find their place and crashing down.

"You can't say it's my birthday and you're not drinking in the same sentence, it doesn't even make sense," Drea says.

Chloe raises the glass with everyone else and they all introduce the burning liquids to their throats and she braces for what's to come. Another night filled with one ounce of hell after another after another, numbing the pain before imminently drowning her in it. Laughter with her girls transforms to self-destruction, she picks herself apart from the inside out with a smile on her face and red behind her eyes.

It could be the comparison of her behind the scenes to others' carefully curated performances, but she feels so behind. There is no bright side, there seems to be no finish line, the ladder is never-ending, and with all the work she does it's becoming more apparent she's going nowhere fast while giving everything to go above and beyond. She strives to be seen as exceptional, only to be passed up and pressed down by the inherent privilege of someone who is average at best.

Being a Black woman is her courage and her strength, it has carried her farther than she could often imagine. But the weight of being who she is in spaces created to undervalue and undermine just that is steadily growing too heavy. Every ounce of hell picks her up, then drags her down to their territory. Lower and lower to the enticement of no longer trying, where her sleep sings loudly with tragedy and she questions everything.

***

Chloe waves goodbye from the window and her friends pull off.

The house is quiet and her ears ring. Her heels land on the opposite side of the living room and the cold hardwood floors push back against the bottom of her feet. She dives onto the couch and buries herself in blankets as her mind spins and she curses peer pressure as her subconscious wastes no time with her welcome.

The shadow is heard before seen. Its voice is strong and unforgiving as it taunts her, drawing her further into the darkness. Threats sting through thick whispers and she shudders as the volume grows and the shadow reveals itself more and more.

You don't deserve it. Give it to someone that knows what to do with it. You don't do anything right. Fix all your mistakes... give yourself away.

The insults feel just as real as the tears. Chloe's legs soften and she falls to her knees as the darkness swallows her. It's easier to fall into it all, so that's what she usually does. She lets her face flood with heat and accepts destruction. She'll wake up soon and pretend this never happened, feeding herself another lie that she will never drink again. It's just how these nights go. But this time, the little strength she still has inside does something it's never once done. It screams her name.

She looks up through her widened eyes blurred with tears as a vivid realization appears: this is just a nightmare.

Chloe! The shadow is nothing but the darkest part of you. Reclaim your mind. Now!

Her body rises like a phoenix and the song of tragedy is cut as she finds her voice and directs it toward the shadow. "No! Your words mean nothing. You are nothing! I'm done feeding into you. I am in control of my life! I am in control!"

Her subconscious shakes as she commences its crash with her conviction.

"I am in control! I am in control! I am in control!"

The darkness begins to fade as she bears witness to her own power. Her mind tussles between remaining in the scene and awakening with her new-found dignity. As the darkness fights the light, the shadow approaches closer than it ever has before and its strong voice utters words she's never heard him say. "We'll see about that."

And for the first time Chloe sees its face, striking a fear down her spine that shoots her back to the gray gasping for air. Her chest pushes in and out and her breathing pierces the silence. The image slowly dissolves as her eyes adjust to the morning sunlight and she does her best to let it leave, cursing herself for succumbing to the peer pressure of her friends yet again.

***

Chloe didn't make it to Saturday morning Pilates, but she put on her dad hat and largest sunglasses for brunch. At least the blank stare is hidden.

The table is crowded with her similarly disguised friends, hiding their eyes from the sunshine and washing hangover medication down with lemon water, coffee, and mimosas. The air is filled with recounts of moments barely remembered from a night Chloe wants nothing more than to forget. Her body hurts and her insides have been twisted up all morning. Something is off.

She sips her coffee, and as the mug lowers from her lips, her eyes rise to Drea as she speaks. But as she glances at her friend, she sees the face of the shadow staring back at her.

Chloe shrieks, fear striking down her spine once again as she jumps from her seat, shaking the table and spilling her coffee and sending silence over half the restaurant. Her friends are worried.

Girl, what in the world? Chloe, are you good? What was that?

She points at Drea but the shadow's face is gone just as quickly as it appeared. She's left repeating her friends' questions back to herself in her mind. She would run out of here if her feet weren't nailed to the ground with embarrassment. A man hurries over with a rag and begins to clean up the mess she made. Her cheeks burn. His smile is glazed with sugar and her heartbeat fills her ears. His voice sounds underwater. "Are you okay? I'll have your server bring another coffee right over for you," he walks away before she can answer.

Girl, I think he likes you. He's cute! That's the new manager, he replaced what's-his-face. Chloe, you need to hop on that, you could use some excitement in your life to help you loosen up. You've been extra weird lately, girl, please get your groove back...

On their way out, the manager catches Chloe's eye again. They exchange information and a date is planned for tomorrow before she even makes it to her car.

***

The evening lands and her body feels better but her mind is still out of place.

She feels uneasy, the shadow's face remains at the forefront of her mind and it haunts her. Climbing into bed and closing her eyes, it's the first thing she sees. It usually takes her a while to fall asleep. Her thoughts are usually cluttered with loud anxieties about work and her potential, but tonight she'd give anything to focus on something so miniscule in comparison to being overcome by pure fear. She squeezes her eyes shut, trying to focus on something, anything good. Anything to bring her to a comfortable enough space to let her body rest. And the thought of tomorrow's date comes to mind. The corner of her lips rises as she envisions scenarios of how it may play it out. She imagines his energy and getting lost in his sweet smile. And just as she's drifting to sleep, she is thrown back awake by what sounds like footsteps outside her bedroom.

Chloe swings her feet over the side of the bed and grabs the baseball bat located behind her nightstand in one swift motion. She tiptoes toward the door, and as she approaches, the footsteps on the other side approach too. She grips the weapon harder and takes a deep breath, wishing this was just a dream, hoping it's just the old wooden floors of her house playing tricks on her. And she counts to three.

One... two...

She swings open the door and springs into the hallway, swinging the bat several times before realizing nothing is there. It's just her, fully convinced she is losing her mind.

✳✳✳

Aden doesn't feel like a man she just met.

In the process of getting to know him, it actually feels as if she is digging deeper into herself. Maybe her friends were right... this is what she's been needing.

They've been practically inseparable since the first date. His presence brings her a peace she's never known. His words are always right and on time, urging her to look further within herself and placing the stars back in her eyes. She's grown to strongly dislike not being around him. Not only because of how full she feels beside him, but because of how strange things continue to be when she's alone. Once she considers telling him about what she's been seeing and hearing, the face of the shadow man appearing in real life, the footsteps outside her bedroom door at night, he already says what she needs to hear.

"I'm here for you. I want nothing more than to see you be the best you can be," he says. And she believes him.

Chloe waves goodbye from her window and Aden drives off. It's time for her to really figure out what's wrong, so she calls the perfect person to help.

"Hey Baby," her aunt answers the phone. "What's going on?"

Still floating on a high, Chloe tells the woman that raised her about Aden.

"He sounds like just the nicest gentleman," her aunt says. "I'm excited to watch this unfold. This might be the man of your dreams. Set your intentions for the relationship and stick to them."

"Yes, Auntie."

Everything her aunt does is done with spiritual intention. She has always tried to instill the same practices in Chloe, but Chloe has never picked up on energies with the same efficacy as her aunt. She always misses something, meanwhile her aunt rarely misses. She can spot a kindred spirit and a bag vibe from miles away, and is savvy with the cleansing of negative energies with nothing more than a strong and willing mind. Chloe tells her everything that's been happening, from the dream to the hallucinations to the noises.

"Baby, I'll be honest. It sounds like the entity from your dream has attached itself to you and has been for some years now. I love that you tried to assert your dominance in that nightmare, but you're still living and working at a low frequency. The negative space you've been in mentally is the cause, and the alcohol you drank that night was a catalyst for the attachment. The entity was able to assert its dominance right back, overpowering you and actually entering your world. That's why you're seeing and hearing things. He's here."

"*He's here?* What does that mean? The shadow is... real?"

"Yes and no," her aunt says. "I need you to do several very important things, Baby. Pay close attention to the people around you. If anyone makes you question their motives, ask them 'who are you?'. If they contain that entity, they'll either have to admit it, stating exactly who they are, or completely remove themselves from your world. Also, raise your vibration. No more negative self-talk and being down on yourself. You're weakening the shield of your soul to the point entities like these can latch onto you. I don't want to scare you, but this is dangerous. I'm not sure the shadow has good intentions. The fact that he went out his way to overpower you suggests otherwise. You need to take back control and do it quickly."

***

Her body is under attack.

Work in the office is done on autopilot, Chloe's mind is restless. It's impossible to think about anything outside of what is happening to her.

She proceeds to make plans with every woman in her friend group and she watches them closely. Her heart skips at the thought of trusting anyone trying to steal her life. It's painful to stay calm.

Night after night, it's harder to sleep. Every successful dozing off is followed closely by the footsteps, no longer stopping outside of her door, but now pacing from the far corner of her room to the foot of her bed. Her aunt tells her it's imperative not to fall into fear. All the shadow can do is be near her. As long as Chloe does what she's supposed to do, it will all come to an end soon. So, she keeps the television on with the volume high to try and drown out the sound of what is currently outside of her control. Fatigue can make her weak and more vulnerable, so she creates solace under the covers, forcing herself to return to visions of glitter and eventually falling asleep. No more negative self-talk, no more destruction, no more pessimism. Her life is on the line in more ways than one.

Weeks pass and there's been no luck in revealing the vessel the shadow man is utilizing. No one makes Chloe question their motives, they all continue to be who they've always been. Her friends are insane but loving, her co-workers cordial but distant. Every evening, she arrives home, kicks her shoes across the living room floor, lands on the couch and tries not to spiral.

"Baby, I'm sorry. I didn't mean to scare you," her aunt says through the phone. "Here, take this night to relax as best you can. It's Friday and you've been stressing over this situation to no end. Do whatever makes you feel good and make a point to remove all these wild thoughts from your mind. You're absolutely feeding the shadow by constantly thinking about him. Let loose. Focus on raising your spirit. He'll be forced to back off a bit more until you're able to catch him. You hear me? Stay strong. Listen to me. Don't give up on yourself."

"I hear you, Auntie."

***

Wooden wicks chuckle in the corner of every room, and the melodies of smooth jazz from the wireless speaker make the fires dance. A bubble bath is drawn and tea is brewed. She moisturizes her body with oils from head to toe, breathing in the scent of lavender and feeling the weight of her body lift. She wraps her golden brown skin in a black satin robe, and the doorbell rings right on time.

Aden stands at her doorstep with a bouquet of assorted flowers and that glazed smile. She couldn't have a perfect night of relaxation without him.

They cuddle with each other and their goals, her couch now a safe haven with his protective aura sharing the space. She melts into him, releasing all inhibitions and so naturally doing what her aunt instructed her to do without even thinking about it. They talk and they sit in silence and their connection grows deeper. This man has grown to mean so much to her in so little time and all she wants to do is keep diving more into who he is.

"Aden, who are you? It's like you're an angel sent here just for me. I almost can't even believe it."

He is silent and she raises herself from his chest to turn and face him. The sweet smile trembles just enough to make her frown. Then she realizes what she mistakenly asked him.

Who are you?

She puts some space between them and he moves toward her.

"I am a part of you," he finally says. "This isn't a regular connection. I know you haven't experienced anything like this before, and I haven't either. I know all your thoughts and feelings before you even tell me, and I just want to take all your pain and worries away and carry them for you. I want to make it all better for you. Will you let me do that?"

Chloe is surprised. Pleasantly.

She couldn't have imagined a better answer, a better outcome. He is exactly who he says he is and she's in love. He would do anything for her, and now she knows she would do anything for him. "Yes," she answers. "You don't understand how much this means to me. You've saved me from myself by simply being you."

"No, I don't think you know how much this means to me."

They share a kiss and Chloe feels their souls combine. She feels his spirit embracing hers.

"Let me take control," he whispers. And she lets go. She lets go of all the stress and headaches. All the negativity and worries. She lets go of everything that is not within this moment. All she needs is right here.

***

Her eyes flutter open to the morning sunlight. The bedroom is quiet besides the faint sound of birds chirping outside the window. She smiles and stretches, well-rested and alone in the middle of her bed. Then the phone rings and she notices the time is well after noon.

"Hey Baby. How was your night? Did you do what I told you?"

"Hey, Auntie. Yes, I did and it was just what I needed. Thank you."

"Perfect. You should be nice and recharged. You'll find the shadow in no time."

"That won't be an issue anymore, Auntie. I took care of it."

"Oh?"

"Yes. I showed her who's really in control. Things will be much different now. Life will be much better," Her aunt remains quiet over the line. "Are you still there, Auntie?"

"Who are you?" Her aunt finally asks.

A smile forms on Chloe's face. "It's me, Auntie. Removed from the shadows. Don't worry about a thing. The right one is in control now."

A. ERIN WALKER was born and raised in Cleveland, Ohio. She is also the author of AWAY, FRAGILE, and the DRIVE series: DRIVE and ARRIVE.

For updates on books, events, and more:
www.aerinwalker.com
Goodreads: aerinwalker
Facebook: A. Erin Walker
Pinterest: aerinwalkerwrites
Instagram: a.erinw